ELIZA DOUGLAS

Evernight Teen ®

www.evernightteen.com

ELIZA DOUGLAS

HIS STAR

Eliza Douglas

Copyright © 2023

❧ ⋯ ◆ ⋯ ❧

Chapter One

Cody

The all-consuming darkness of the concert venue was intense until the bright sharp glare of a single blinding spotlight began to scan the stage. The light was probing, acting like a search beacon hunting for its prey. The white beam zoned in and fixed its dazzling brilliance on Cody. He was trapped. The faces of Trend's fans were focused on him, and this was his moment to shine.

With drumsticks suspended high in the air above his head, he was using only the foot pedal for sound as he beat out a heavy bass rhythm on the drum kit. Pounding hard, he managed to produce a repetitive pulsating thud that was a solid hypnotic *toof, toof, dada da, toof.*

The noise was captivating and the vibrations coming from the drums were sure to hit everyone hard in the gut as they rippled over the swaying mass of bodies. The music he played for Trend was like nothing he'd produced before, but somehow, it got the crowd up and swaying to its beat every time.

With one smooth-flowing action, Cody brought his drumsticks down hard onto the taut skins of his drums. Slamming the oak wood of his sticks from one drum to the next in a cyclical tempo, a resounding noise echoed around the concert chamber. He had no idea how he managed to capture the audience's attention during the gig, all he knew was that when he played, people were drawn in and mesmerized by his music.

Every time he worked his magic and the crowd swayed to the beat, he got that indescribable feeling, an unexpected rush of euphoria, that gave him a sense of hope that perhaps he wasn't a failure after all. Perhaps there was a chance that someday in the not-too-distant future, he could make it in the world of entertainment as a true musician.z

There was a break in the music, just after the intro and just before the lyrics of the song started, when someone in the darkness of the crowd shouted out, trying to attract his attention.

"Hey, Cody. Give it to us again. Come on, man. Let's hear it one more time."

"Yeah. Like now…" called another.

Cody glanced across the stage to the other four band members of Trend. They were seasoned musicians accustomed to the cries from the crowd asking for a repeat of the intro, but Cody wasn't. He was new to the group. So new, that when the band member's nodded, it took a few seconds before he realized they were giving him the go-ahead. They expected him to play the intro again.

Lifting his sticks, he let rip once more, and following his lead, the band joined in. When the song came to an end and the sea of listeners fell silent as the last sweet note of Brent's acoustic guitar lingered in the air, the band knew they had given what they had been asked for. They had given everything from their hearts. They had shared their music, shared their sweat, and they were now being rewarded by a deafening roar of hands coming together, offering the sound of continuous applause.

At nineteen, Cody was the youngest and the newest member of Trend. They were a five-piece band. Mitch, their lead singer, fronted the group. Two players were on guitars. Brent on an acoustic and Sam teasing the strings of an electric guitar, and the group was completed with Holly playing percussion and Cody on drums.

Cody always sat half-hidden behind the protective shield of his drum kit, which was where he liked to be … tucked away, and out of the limelight. As much as he enjoyed being with the guys and playing for a crowd, he was really there for the music. Music was his life, it always had been, and he just loved the process of creating songs.

Placing his guitar on its stand, Brent strolled over and stood close to Cody's drum kit, and mouthed, "We're done for the night. Now let's get out of here."

"Are you sure?" he asked. He wiped the beads of sweat from his brow with the back of his arm.

It might be a bit premature to shut down the sound equipment.

Mitch tapped a couple of fingers on the mic's wire mesh grille and blew a few puffs of breath across it. He was testing the microphone and the distorted sound that emerged gave the impression he was preparing to start another song.

Brent lifted his shoulders in an uncaring shrug. "After a two-hour stint on stage, I'm heading to the dressing room even if you guys aren't."

Following Brent's lead, with a final flourish and a

wave to their fans, the five of them headed backstage to where their manager, Paul, was waiting in their dressing room. Towels and refreshments were at the ready. Nutritional drinks and protein-packed fruit bars were on hand to boost their energy, and exhausted from performing on stage, they all needed a sugar boost to get their energy levels up and running again.

Glancing around the cluttered dressing room, Cody still had to pinch himself when he thought about where he was and what was happening to him.

Two months ago, he'd been at college studying economics, and now he was drumming for Trend. It was luck. Pure luck that he'd been offered the job as a drummer and he wasn't about to walk away from the chance of stardom.

****

On the night he'd met the band members of Trend for the first time, he had been downtown in a local club, sitting at the bar with friends, drinking. As the evening progressed, they had become deep in conversation. They had talked mainly about the future and where they were all heading, career-wise.

For most of the academic year, Cody had been thinking about taking a gap year away from learning. He'd come to a crossroads in his life and was trying to decide if he ought to stick to the college course and complete his degree or perhaps pursue other interests. He'd been thrashing over his choices with his mates but came to the decision that perhaps the club hadn't been the best place to have a conversation of such in-depth magnitude. There were too many distractions.

That evening, the club had been holding an open microphone session and there was quite a crowd at the venue. At least a couple of hundred bodies.

Three guys and a girl had been on a small podium

tuning instruments and looking as if they were about to play. At one point, they'd shouted toward the crowd, explaining they were short of a drummer and asked if anyone could play the drums and fancied having a go to help them out.

With a few beers under his belt, although he was by no means drunk, Cody had raised his hand upward as if reaching for the stars and his dreams. And then, encouraged by his friends and with an ease that had surprised him, he'd been jostled and sort of crowd-surfed in the direction of the stage until he'd reached the podium.

Fast-forward two months, and with plenty of performances behind him, he was now officially a member of Trend and about to go on tour with the band.

****

With the gig over and once again backstage and in their dressing room, Mitch claimed the old threadbare sofa and crashed. Mitch always got to the sofa first. No matter how hard the others tried, they always seemed to lose out. Eventually, they had more or less come to accept Mitch was the guy all the girls chased after, and that he was the one that had the first pick of all the perks.

"Are you coming with us?" Holly asked, looking across the dressing room at Cody.

The room was a mess. Suitcases, worn music cases, and a collection of clothes were strewn about the place, and she was busy trying to gather her things together.

"I think I'll give it a miss tonight." Cody yawned.

He was whacked. The muscles in his arms and back ached where he'd been crouched over his drum kit, beating out a rhythm. He felt like his spine could snap in half at the lightest touch. He was tense and needed to unwind and relax. It had been a long grueling day and there was an even longer week of work stretching ahead of him. He still had things to do. Things that couldn't be put off ... like finishing that new song he was writing and FaceTiming his parents.

Stupid as it seemed, at nineteen, he ought to be his own man, but he still had an inner emotional need to check in with his parents. Not because he had to, but because he wanted to. When he'd joined the band and left college, it was also with the understanding that he would touch base with them on a regular basis. They cared about him, and in return, he cared about them too.

"Are you sure you won't come with us tonight?" Holly swayed her hips flirtatiously. His lips widened into a smile and he shook his head. He knew her come-on wasn't serious. She already had a steady boyfriend. "We're going to Jamerson's for an hour or two. Just to unwind and let off steam and maybe dance. You know what it's like. After a performance, you either want to collapse and go to bed, or you want to party. Tonight, I feel like getting smashed. I haven't got pissed, you know, completely blotto, in weeks."

Cody never really partied. And he'd certainly never wanted to get so drunk that he didn't know what he was doing. He didn't have an extrovert personality like Holly. He was a bit of a loner, which was why so many of his friends were surprised he was a musician playing in a group.

Occasionally he asked a girl out and had taken her to a club, but he'd never been a real hard party animal ... not like Mitch.

If Mitch saw his bed before three in the morning it was the exception rather than the rule. And if in the morning there happened to be a girl sharing Mitch's bed, no one batted an eyelid anymore. The band had become used to the way their lead singer lived. It was just that

Cody hadn't decided if he wanted to cultivate that sort of hard-rock star image. He supposed it was something fans expected, but he wasn't sure it was for *him*, or something he truly wanted to do.

Having fans flock to see him because he was a rock star wasn't what Cody was after. Trend wasn't exactly famous, but after appearing on a guest spot in a TV show, their social media accounts had been swamped with followers and comments, and it felt as if they were on their way to stardom. But Cody wasn't after stardom. He just wanted recognition for being a great musician, and an amazing drummer.

"Come on." Holly smiled like she was trying to persuade him. "You might see someone you like for a change and you might even connect. Although, if I didn't already have a boyfriend, even I might be tempted to seduce you."

Cody laughed. The thought of him and Holly being together *in that way* was absurd. She was pretty, with golden curly hair and a petite body, and some might say even beautiful, but she didn't stir his senses. They were friends and of course bandmates.

He supposed he was no different from other guys his age. He'd been on a few dates and tested the waters so to speak, but until now, he'd never really had a serious long-term girlfriend. Something always seemed to be missing.

Cody had been chasing his dream of being a drummer, and not chasing the girls, or trying to get them into bed.

It was the small things that made him begin to think that perhaps he could have feelings for his own sex. For one thing, he found guys more attractive to look at than girls. He liked to see a guy in tight jeans and wasn't at all turned on by female boobs and asses. He'd always said it was a girl's mind that he found attractive, but now he was beginning to wonder if he was waiting for the right guy to come along, and if perhaps he was gay.

Holly came over to where he was standing and wrapped her arms around his waist. "I think you ought to make an effort. It might be the last chance you get to let your hair down for a few weeks. With our gig in Amsterdam on the horizon, you ought to make the most of the chance to have a good time. You never know when we'll next be let out to play. When we're on tour, I doubt Paul will let us out of his sight."

A few days ago, Paul Canton, their manager, had said something about booking a concert in Amsterdam, but Cody had thought nothing definite had been agreed upon.

It seemed he was wrong.

If Holly was already planning a trip to Holland, then the concert in Amsterdam must have been booked.

"What do you know about Amsterdam that I don't?" Cody asked.

Holly stepped away from him, nonchalantly flicked her hair back from her face, and shrugged. "Nothing really. Only what Paul told us this morning before you got here." She looked in a nearby mirror and something caught her attention. Wetting her finger with a drop of moisture from her tongue, she wiped a smudge of black mascara away from beneath her eye. "Paul has never suggested anything like this before," she said. "I sort of got the feeling that something was definitely happening. He wouldn't hint at going to Amsterdam if it wasn't more or less in the cards."

"I suppose you know what you're talking about," Cody said. "After all, you've been with the band longer than I have, so I assume you'd know if there was a gig happening."

Cody wasn't sure about packing his bags and leaving England. Of course, he'd been to Europe on several occasions for vacation, but it had been with his parents. They had always gone as a family. He'd never been in a situation like this before where he would be on his own. True, he'd be going with the band and their manager would also be on hand to organize things, but it wasn't the same. He would be doing things alone and looking out for himself … single-handedly. And besides that, he wasn't sure he was mature enough to handle the pressure of making his own decisions. His parents had always been there to support him and act as a sounding board—no matter what he decided to do.

If he was honest, he knew they hadn't been completely happy about him leaving college and joining Trend. But they had said it was his life and that he had to learn to make his own mistakes and deal with whatever came his way … and he was doing just that.

Having said good night to Holly and the other band members, Cody started to make his way back to his one-bedroom flat in Kensington. Apart from small groups of people spilling out from the local pubs after an evening of drinking, London's streets were deserted. At two in the morning, if any normal person was about, the one thing they had on their mind was to crawl home and find their beds—only Cody wasn't heading home to his bed.

Although tired and exhausted from playing, he was too keyed up to sleep. It often happened after a gig. And that night, with the adrenaline pumping through his body, he knew he would be unable to rest, and the only cure for his insomnia would be to go for a jog.

A run around Hyde Park always helped. After a quick sprint and with his excess energy sapped, he generally managed to fall into a deep sleep that lasted well into the morning.

But Cody hadn't planned to go jogging, and he didn't have his jogging gear with him. He was wearing his old denims and a pair of well-worn trainers, and he decided they would have to do. With nothing and no one to stop him, he set off for Hyde Park.

The night air had a bite to it. It was cold but not too cold. And having jogged a few laps on the tarmac pathway that circled the murky black water of the lake, he was about to call it a night and head for his bed, when he noticed something moving near the boathouse. It was dark, too dark to see clearly, but as the old Victorian lampposts blazed a soft trail of light down to the boathouse, he could just make out a small cluster of people gathered near the water's edge.

The hazy outlines of four youths could be seen lurking about near the landing stage. It was where the boats were kept tied up during the day in readiness for the public to use. Only it wasn't daytime… it was night. And at night, everything was supposed to be securely locked away in the wooden boathouse.

What was the group of youths up to, and why were they there? Cody thought something wasn't right. It seemed sinister.

Chapter Two

Cody

Slowing his speed, Cody came to a halt. His heart was beating fast and he could feel his blood pounding through his veins. With his hands resting on his hips, he took deep breaths and tried to regain control of his labored breathing. He was short on air and panting.

When studying at college, he'd been super fit. He'd been on the athletics track team and he'd run the five-hundred meters sprint, only now, not having kept up his training, he was out of practice and it showed.

Taking the chilled summer night air deep into his lungs, he eventually gained control of his breathing and with hesitant steps, he moved closer to the group.

"Is everything all right?" he called out. He was a safe distance away from them. Safe enough, that if there was any trouble, he could leg it out of there.

"We're fine," someone shouted back. "No need for you to worry."

Cody was reluctant to get involved. He wasn't looking for trouble. But something warned him that all wasn't right. A sense of unease surfaced.

"Are you sure? I mean…" He took a step closer then stopped.

"Look, we said we're okay. Now clear off." The tone of voice was aggressive.

Thinking what was going on was none of his business, Cody was about to turn away when he heard a faint sound of a muffled cry for help. Someone was struggling to break free from the group and Cody instinctively knew danger was in front of him, but he didn't know what sort of danger it was.

Beneath the orange glow of the park's regimented

street lamps, attracted by the glare of the light, white moths danced with death. And on the grass verge at the side of the lake, with their heads tucked securely under their wings, was a smattering of ducks and swans, hiding from the long shadows of the night. But no other human was in sight—just these guys and their *victim*.

"Hey, look…" Cody took a few steps forward. Was he an idiot? What was he doing there? He couldn't help anyone. He was outnumbered. Perhaps he ought to turn and run before it was too late for him to back away. But he couldn't. "I can either call the cops or you can let your … um … friend go."

With the bright glow of the moon bouncing off the water, shining behind the group, a clearer outline of a youth struggling to break free could be seen. Two guys were holding him by the wrists and arms, and it looked like the third guy had been using the victim as a punching bag. Cody couldn't back away now, could he? It wasn't in his nature to leave someone who was asking for help. The stifled muffled cries were heard again.

If Cody's calculations were right, there were three attackers. Perhaps with the victim's help, they might just manage to overpower the thugs. He knew he was outnumbered and the odds of doing any good were stacked against him, but he had to try.

He had nothing on him that could act as a defensive weapon, and then, out of the corner of his eye, he saw a rescue lifebuoy. It was a red and white ring with a rope attached, and it was fixed onto a stand that was close to the lake in case someone fell into the water.

The buoy was the only thing to hand and Cody knew what he had to do. It was now or never. He had to decide to act or simply walk away.

Under normal circumstances, confrontation of any sort wasn't his style, but this wasn't normal … was it? A group of lads beating someone up wasn't what happened in real life, or at least not in Cody's world.

Going over to the stand, he removed the ring from its securing hook. With the lifebuoy held tight in his grasp, he walked with determined strides toward the youths.

Taking a deep breath, he repeated, "I said, let him go."

"Fuck off," was the sharp retort.

Was that a glint, a flash of a steel blade?

Then slowly, with a steady swinging motion and with his arms extended, Cody began to sway the heavy lifebuoy ring from one side of his body to the other. He was like a discus thrower preparing to launch a lethal weapon. Only he wasn't planning to release the lifebuoy aimlessly into the air. He was going to aim it and strike out at the attackers and hopefully hit his target.

As he advanced toward the youths, even under the cloak of darkness, he was able to witness a look of surprise on their faces. Something like disbelief appeared. It was clear they hadn't expected any opposition to their nocturnal pleasure-seeking adventure, but Cody was there, and he was prepared to fight.

"Let him go..." Cody threatened. Nothing happened.

The struggling victim was still held fast and the leader of the thugs hadn't made a move to lower his clenched fist or let the victim go. And then the sound of flesh-on-flesh could be heard as the menacing fist landed against the side of the unwilling recipient's face.

Cody lashed out, and as the lifebuoy made contact with a thug's chest, the guy doubled over, gasping for breath.

While one man was down, Cody took stock, and using the lifebuoy's rope that was clenched tight in his hand, like a lasso, he retrieved the ring and aimed for a different thug. He had the advantage of surprise. A second hit landed and another thug buckled from the blow of the lifebuoy which meant two thugs were down.

"Come on, let's get out of here and leave the fucking faggots to get better acquainted. Only faggots and queers are in the park at night. Anyway, we've got what we wanted, let's get out of here." It was the third thug, the one that was still standing and hadn't been hit that had spoken.

Cody saw something like a wallet or an iPhone being flashed tauntingly before the victim's eyes. And then the three attackers ran off, heading in the direction of the park's tall iron gates before vanishing into the mangled maze of London's streets.

****

Cody went to where the wounded casualty had collapsed. He was no longer being held in place by the brutal ruffians as they beat him. He had sunk to his knees, crumbling like a rag doll, defeated. The youth seemed dazed, in shock, and completely defenseless.

Cody reached out offering comfort, but all he got was a frightened rejection. The boy recoiled cowering away from his outstretched hand as if Cody was the enemy.

"It's all right. They've gone." Cody tried to reassure him, but he wasn't certain the message was getting across. "I'm not going to hurt you."

Behind dark-rimmed glasses that sat awkwardly on his nose, and with eyes that were wide and fearful, the boy looked up. His teeth were chattering vigorously against one another and his body was shivering. Cody didn't know if it was because of the frightening experience or if it was because the boy was wearing only jeans and a t-shirt, and the summer night air was chilled.

"Are you sure it's okay now? Have they really gone?"

Reaching down, Cody wrapped an arm around the boy hoping to offer comfort and some body warmth. Careful not to hurt, he pulled the injured survivor to his feet and looped one of his bruised arms about his own shoulders for support.

Shit, Cody thought. *They've beaten him black and blue.*

There was hardly any flesh on him. He was tall, lanky, and thin. Too thin for Cody's liking, and it looked as if he hadn't had a good meal in weeks. Asian men and women tended to be delicate in stature and quiet in nature, but this wasn't normal. The boy hadn't offered a word of complaint even though his velvety-brown skin looked badly battered.

Cody had no idea how the boy had survived the beating he'd been given ... but thankfully he had, and now it was a question of getting him to safety.

"They're gone, or at least I can't see them in the park. So, for now, I think it's safe to make a move, but you never know, they might return."

"I hope not. It was really my fault I got beaten. I shouldn't have come to the park in the first place, but—"

"Look, I think we really ought to get out of here. They might turn around and come back to look for us. Can you walk or should I leave you here and go for help?"

Cody had bluffed when he'd told the thugs he would call the cops. He didn't have his iPhone on him. He never went jogging with anything heavy in his pockets. And an iPhone would have fallen out of his jeans, so he never carried one.

Together, they took a step forward and Cody heard the muffled sound of a sharp intake of breath as a reaction to pain.

"No, please don't leave. I wouldn't feel safe if you left me alone."

"What's your name?" Cody asked.

A few more steps and they had moved away from the boathouse and were back on the park's meandering concrete pathway.

"Aki. My name is Aki Ch—"

Aki broke off and gave another groan of discomfort. Cody wasn't sure if it was a sharp pain that had caused Aki to stop in the middle of revealing his identity, or if it was simply the fact that he had something to hide. But Cody didn't want to push his luck. If Aki was scared, he didn't want to alarm him further by performing a cross-examination.

"Cody Freeman, at your service." Cody adjusted his hold on Aki, and even though Aki was skinny, Cody had to more or less support his full weight. "Come on. Let's get you to the hospital and get you looked over. And while we're there, I'll ask the doctors if they can report the mugging to the police."

"No … no hospitals and especially no police," Aki said hurriedly.

Aki was on edge and Cody wondered why. Was he in some sort of trouble?

"I'll be fine." Aki winced. "And I don't need you to mother me. I'm old enough to look after myself."

"And how old is that?"

A moment ago, like a baby, Aki had been pleading not to be left alone in the park and now he was accusing Cody of mothering him.

"Let's just say I'm old enough to make my own decisions and leave it at that."

"But you look…"

"Don't worry. I'll survive. I might only be

seventeen now, but I'll be eighteen in a couple of months and I can look after myself. I've always had to. Anyway, those guys didn't do any major damage. They stole my phone and that's about it."

"But they were hitting you."

"It's just a few bruises and I don't think anything's broken, although my ribs do hurt."

"Even if nothing's broken, I think you ought to be checked over. Or at least report what's happened to the police. They could try and catch those guys and maybe stop them from attacking someone else."

"I said no hospital and no police." Aki was adamant.

With slow, steady steps, they began walking to the main gates of the park. If Aki had been a girl, Cody was sure he would have been tempted to lift her up in his arms and carry her to safety. But he couldn't do that with Aki, could he? Not with a guy. Yet he had the urge to hold Aki and watch over him.

Why was he feeling so protective?

Progress was made and they eventually reached the main road. It was a place where they could hail a taxi cab and Aki could be taken to safety. Only he didn't know where that safe place was. He didn't know if Aki lived alone or with family, but he had said he was seventeen so perhaps he still lived at home with his parents.

They came to a halt at the park gates and Cody wasn't taking another step until he knew what was happening.

"Look…" Cody said, trying to be the grown-up in a situation that was out of his control. "We … I mean *you* have three choices. You can either go to the police station and report the mugging or I can take you home to your parents and leave you there … or…"

"Or what?" Aki asked.

Damn, this was awkward. Cody didn't want to get involved. He was the type of guy that watched from the sidelines to see how others solved their problems, but it seemed he was already in over his head. He couldn't just leave Aki on the streets of London without protection, could he?

Cody took a steadying breath. "I suppose at a push, I can take you back to my place and we can decide what's going to happen from there. It will also give you a chance to clean up and I'll have an opportunity to look at your wounds."

There, he had done it. Against his better judgment, he was taking responsibility for another human being and there was no going back. He was stuck with Aki.

"Then it will have to be your place. I'm not going to my parents' home looking like this. Tom and Jerry would go ballistic, and they might even be that now if they've discovered I'm not at the house. And as for going to the police, that's out of the question. The press would have a field day if they found out I'd walked into a police station to report a crime."

"Who are Tom and Jerry, and what do you mean … the press? How would they be involved?"

"It's a long story and something you don't need to worry about for now. Let's just say that over the next couple of weeks, with holidays kicking in, no one will miss me, especially my parents. And as for telling the cops and the press about what happened tonight, the less they know the better."

Cody didn't delve deeper. The time wasn't right to find out what Aki meant.

"Then my place it is," he said. "It's only a short distance, so we ought to be able to make it."

Cody hoped he was right about getting Aki safely back to his flat as he looked to be in a bad way.

Chapter Three

Aki

Aching from head to toe, Aki was exhausted from the intense battering he'd just endured. With dogged determination, he navigated the lamplit streets of London and walked beside Cody until they came to a large, elegant Georgian terraced house that was situated down one of the side streets. It was the kind of house affluent trading merchants used to live in—only now, they were occupied by students or little old ladies with Zimmer frames.

"Is this all yours?" Aki asked.

It was a beautiful sandstone building with an uncluttered elegant façade and had steps that led up to a wide front door.

"No, not all of it. I rent the basement apartment," Cody explained. "I've signed a lease for a year, but maybe sometime in the future when I've made my fortune, I'll buy something like this."

Aki frowned and shook his head in despair. "Why is everyone so obsessed with making money? My parents are—"

Aki had been about to reveal to Cody that his parents were multimillionaires, but something stopped him just in time. Cody wasn't to know that having massive amounts of money to spend only meant trouble. Because of his parents' wealth, they lived in a bubble, isolated from the real world. Mainly because once it was known they were rich, all anyone ever wanted from them was a free ride.

"Yes? Your parents are what?" Cody asked.

"Oh, nothing." Aki shrugged. "At least it's nothing important."

Aki was thankful Cody let his last comment slide. He didn't want to explain about his parents and their need to focus on work, 24/7. Their constant goal was to make money and then even more money. They could never get enough.

They were already wealthy beyond imagination and Aki couldn't understand their obsession to fill their coffers at the cost of everything and everyone around them. He believed some things were more important than affluence.

Being born with a silver spoon in your mouth and moving with the seasons from one luxury home to another didn't always mean you were happy, as he knew all too well from experience.

Leaning on Cody's firm body for support, he managed to make it down the steep basement steps until they reached the door to the apartment. The solid bulk of Cody's athletic body was pressed against his and Aki realized just how fit Cody was. Not only did he look and smell good, but he also felt good. The type of guy Aki secretly fancied and longed for but had never dared touch!

"Welcome to what used to be the servants' quarters." Cody extracted a house key from a money belt he had wrapped around his waist. "It's nothing special. My parents live on the outskirts of London. But this place is really just somewhere for me to stay while I'm working. I like it, mainly because it's conveniently located and handy for getting around Central London. And the neighborhood isn't too bad, either … well, except for Hyde Park at night of course."

Turning the key, Cody put his shoulder against the doorjamb and pushed. Running his hand along the wall, he found the light switch, and with a sharp upward flick of his finger, the hallway was flooded with a soft, warm, welcoming light.

Aki looked around. "Nice," he said.

He hoped he didn't sound too negative. It was always difficult commenting on someone's personal decor when that taste didn't necessarily match your own.

At his parents' house, Aki's bedroom was fitted out with every mod-con available. There was a wide-screen TV and surround sound equipment that had great acoustics. He was into electronics and astronomy, so his walls were plastered with images of the solar system and the planets. Bookshelves were weighted down with textbooks and his desk housed his laptop and various project reports he was working on, but Cody's place sort of looked like an old man's home. A bit dull. A bit conservative. And a bit dated. At one end of the room near the window was a cream-colored futon and beside it was an old-fashioned armchair along with a ring-stained coffee table. They were arranged as a sitting area near the TV and at the other end of the room was a small kitchenette space for cooking and eating. The flat was a typical London studio apartment. Dull.

A jumbled collection of takeaway cartons and what looked like the remains of a Korma curry were still on the dining table, and in the sink was a small pile of dishes waiting to be washed. It wasn't a huge pile of crockery, but it would be enough to cause Cassie, their maid at home, to roll up her sleeves and load the dishwasher.

"The place comes already furnished," Cody explained. "Some of the things are mine, but most of the furniture belongs to the landlord. It is what it is. It's somewhere to stay and, well, it's basic."

Out of the corner of his eye, Aki spotted a drum kit. "Do you play?"

"You could say that," Cody gave a lopsided grin

and then walked to a door that was to the side of the kitchenette. He opened it. "Take a seat while I fetch the first aid kit from the bathroom."

Aki played the guitar but he'd always thought that learning to play the drums was something he might like to try when he was older and had a place of his own.

In junior high school, when he had to pick a musical instrument to learn, his parents had thought drums would make too much noise, so they had pushed for him to learn the guitar. A guitar could be plugged into a speaker and the music fed through a headset causing no disturbance to the household. Which had been a major plus in the eyes of his mom and dad.

Instead of taking a seat as Cody had told him to do, he followed Cody into the bathroom. Which might have been the wrong move on his part. The bathroom was small. It had all the essentials, like a toilet, a sink, and a shower, but being in the confined space was a tight fit and brought them close together. Practically body to body.

Standing on tiptoes, Cody was rummaging in a mirrored medicine cabinet above the sink. He didn't seem bothered by Aki's nearness.

Nice ass, Aki thought.

"I think I might have to wash some of this mud and dirt off before you can put a Band-Aid on my cut," Aki said.

Cody turned and looked. "Yep, I think you could be right. It's only a trickle of blood, but I'd prefer to get that cut above your eye cleaned and covered before it gets infected." Once again Cody dived into the cabinet to search for something, and then having found what he was looking for, he flashed a box of Band-Aids in front of Aki. "I'm afraid this is the extent of my first aid kit."

"It's fine. I don't need much, just…" He glanced

down and pulled his grubby t-shirt away from his body. "Would it be all right if I took a shower? It's been a couple of days since I last had one and…"

"Sure. Of course. Get undressed and I'll leave you to it. Fresh towels are on that rack, and if you don't mind using my soap and shampoo, help yourself. I'll wait for you in the other room."

After Cody left, Aki began to strip. He couldn't believe his luck. Not only had Cody come to his rescue in the park when the thugs had cornered him, but Cody was also offering the use of his bathroom to freshen up.

Aki was naked when the bathroom door was pushed slightly open and a hand appeared clutching a bundle of clothes. The clothes were dropped carelessly onto the floor and the door was closed again.

"I thought you might want something clean to change into," Cody called out from behind the closed door. "You can't put your dirty clothes back on, can you? And sorry. The jeans might be a bit on the large size, but they're all I can offer. If there's anything else you need, give me a shout."

How about joining me in the shower and giving me a back rub? Aki wanted to say. But he didn't. He wasn't brave enough … yet!

"Thanks, Cody."

Chapter Four

Aki

Having showered and dressed, Aki went back to the sitting room where Cody was busy in the kitchenette. It looked like Cody had made a pot of coffee and a couple of toasted sandwiches.

"I'm hungry, even if you're not," Cody said. "Come sit down and eat. You can tell me all about what happened in the park while we tuck in."

Thinking about it, Aki realized he was hungry. He hadn't eaten since he'd left his parents' house that morning. Cassie had received strict instructions to look after him while his parents were away and she had offered to cook him breakfast, but he had opted for a bowl of cereal and a glass of fruit juice instead. Some mornings before college, he didn't want a heavy meal. He just grabbed something light and made a dash for the waiting taxi that drove him a couple of blocks from his parents' home in Knightsbridge to his college. But that morning he'd skipped classes, wasting the money his parents had spent on his expensive private education.

"Even if it's three in the morning, shouldn't you call your mom and dad? Just to let them know you're okay and not lying dead somewhere?" Cody asked, sounding concerned. "They'll probably be worried about you."

Aki gave a short harsh laugh. "You don't know my mother and father. They won't be worried. And anyway, they're not in the UK at the moment. They flew to New York last week and haven't been in touch since."

"Then who looks after you while they're away? Surely, they wouldn't have left you on your own?"

"Cassie, our maid, she sort of keeps an eye on me,

but as it's Friday, she won't realize I'm not home until Monday. When my parents are out of the country, she usually has the weekends off. She goes home to her family and—"

"Shouldn't you call her instead?"

"I can't. In fact, I can't call anyone."

"Why not?"

"At the park, when I was attacked, they took my phone. There was nothing really on it. Nothing serious like bank details. Just a few friends' phone numbers and a couple of apps."

"Look, it's been a long day, and probably an even longer one for you. What do you say to sleeping on the couch? I've got a sleeping bag you can use, and in the morning, after you've rested, we'll see what we can do about getting you home and getting your phone back."

"Sounds good to me."

Aki was grateful for everything Cody was doing. Cody was a total stranger, and yet he'd done more for him in the last hour than all his rich, posh classmates had done during the years he had known them.

With the dishes washed and the sleeping bag unearthed from a cupboard, Aki and Cody were ready to hit the sack.

"Are you sure you'll be able to sleep?" Cody asked.

"I'll be fine. But I'll be even better if I can give you a 'thank you' hug."

For a moment, Cody hesitated, and then he walked toward Aki and opened his arms wide.

"Sure. Why not?" Cody said.

It felt so right to be held in Cody's arms. He felt warm and safe.

Cody had gone to bed, leaving the bedroom door slightly ajar, and as Aki lay huddled in the sleeping bag on the makeshift bed in the sitting room, he stretched his aching limbs and yawned contentedly. The light from the table lamp beside the futon cast soft shadows around the room, and as his eyelids closed over his tired eyes, he knew things were going to be all right.

Cody had come to his rescue and the future didn't seem so grim. Tomorrow wasn't going to be just another day. It was going to be a day with a difference. Cody was now in his life.

****

Aki thought it must have been the sun shining between the crack in the curtains that had woken him. For a moment, he lay on the futon trying to get his bearings, and then he realized where he was.

Wriggling out of the sleeping bag, he put on his glasses and threw on some clothes, and went over to Cody's bedroom, but there was no sign of him there. The bed was empty and so was the flat.

Cody was nowhere to be seen.

Dressed and thinking of leaving a thank-you note for Cody before exiting the flat, Aki heard the key turn in the lock and the front door open. Cody entered carrying two thermos cups of coffee and a large brown paper bag.

"Breakfast." Cody smiled triumphantly as if he'd just achieved something out of the ordinary. "I don't usually go out and fetch breakfast, but as I didn't have anything for you to eat, I thought I'd run to the deli coffee shop on the corner and bring something back. I hope you like bagels."

At that moment, Aki would have liked anything Cody had brought. Not just because he was hungry and would eat almost anything that was put in front of him, but because he was simply relieved Cody hadn't disappeared without saying goodbye.

"Yes, sure. Bagels are fine."

But it wasn't just bagels. Cody had also bought some ham and a substantial wedge of cheese, and a couple of croissants, along with a carton of juice. It seemed like a feast.

Halfway through the meal, the conversation turned to what had happened the night before.

"Have you thought any more about going to the police?" Cody asked. "You know, to tell them about your iPhone being taken and about being attacked?"

Aki shook his head and tried to avoid Cody's inquisitive stare.

"I told you, I'm reluctant to get the police involved. But I've thought about a solution to my missing phone."

"And that is?"

"Would you mind if I borrowed your iPhone for two minutes? You see, if I dial my number, I might be able to trace my phone. It has a tracker app and I should be able to locate it."

Cody scratched his head and raised his brows. "It's more than likely those thugs have sold it. You'll be lucky if you see it again."

"But it's worth a try. Don't you think?"

Cody went to his charger and removed his cell phone from the docking station.

"How do you know so much about phones and tracking? I rarely use mine and I wouldn't know the first thing about apps. As for social media and gaming … that's not for me. I'm too busy writing songs and creating music with the band."

Aki laughed. "I'm not a whizz kid or a nerdy geek, but I'm studying electrical engineering at college, and tracking is really basic stuff.

"It's all yours." Cody handed over the phone.

"What's your login password?"

"Um … I don't have one. You just swipe left."

Aki swiped left and sure enough, he was straight onto Cody's welcome page.

"You're right. No password? It's telling me London is bright and sunny, and it looks like you have three messages waiting for you. Do you want me to see what they are?"

Cody held out his hand as if expecting the phone to be returned. "No … I thought you wanted to use the phone to find out where yours was. If you're going to snoop into my private life, I'll have the phone back, please."

"Hey, sorry. I didn't mean to pry. Seriously, that's not why I wanted to use your phone. You can have it back if you don't trust me."

Aki offered Cody the phone, but after a brief pause, Cody shook his head.

"It's okay. You can borrow it. It's just that we're still getting to know one another. It might feel as if I've known you for some time, but the reality is, we've only just met."

Aki wondered if Cody felt the same way. Did he feel the deep connection?

With his mind only half concentrating on what he was doing, while the other half was thinking about Cody, Aki's fingers were busy on the touchpad. "I hope you don't mind if I download a tracer app to your phone. I'll delete it when I've finished, but if I can get it to work, the app will help me find my phone. The problem is your signal isn't too great, is it?"

Aki keyed his mobile phone number into Cody's contact data and waited for the app to respond. The blue round arrow was telling him it was busy searching.

Then … bingo! He had tracked his lost phone. It was somewhere in Notting Hill—which wasn't too far from where they were.

Aki looked over the frame of his glasses at Cody and his smile must have said it all.

"I guess you've found your phone," Cody said, coming to the correct conclusion. "What do you want to do? Do you want to see if you can collect the phone or would you prefer to contact the police and see if they'll tackle the problem for you?"

"I'll take a cab and see what I find at the other end. You never know, the person that has my phone might just hand it over without a fight."

"I suppose you'd like me to go with you."

Aki hesitated. Right now, more than anything, he wanted to have Cody at his side, but he realized Cody had a life of his own.

"Look, you probably have other things to do. It wouldn't be fair to ask you to be my wingman. And as much as I'd like you to be there in case something happens…"

"Isn't that what friends are for?" Cody dug his hands deep into the pockets of his jeans. "Friends are supposed to be there to help when there's trouble."

"But we haven't known one another that long."

"Long enough," Cody said. "After what we went through last night, I'd say we're more than friends. In fact, as I practically saved your life, don't you think I'm allowed to find out what happened to your phone and see this thing through to its conclusion?"

"When you put it like that…"

"Besides, I'd like to get a proper look at those thugs in daylight."

Aki was just happy Cody wanted to hang around.

Locking the flat behind them, they managed to flag down a cab and reached Notting Hill in a matter of minutes. Arriving at their destination and with the cab paid, they stood outside a small, trendy café on Portobello Road.

A few tables and chairs were on the pavement underneath a green canopy outside the café. And a couple of people were sitting in the afternoon sunshine reading the Saturday papers while relaxing and drinking their coffees.

It didn't look like a bad area, but Aki never knew what might be waiting for him. Except for last night, he was usually overcautious. It was what his parents had taught him to be. But with Cassie, their housekeeper, away, and having given his bodyguards a fake story about sleeping over at a friend's house, he had ventured out at night and found himself in Hyde Park being mugged.

It was a lesson learned the hard way.

Still holding Cody's phone in his hand, he looked at the screen and noticed the tracker hadn't moved its position.

"It looks like whoever has my phone is still here," Aki said.

In the light of day, he wasn't afraid to tackle the group of thugs. But he was glad Cody was with him, giving moral support.

"Let's go in." Leading the way, Cody pushed the door open.

Inside the café, it was just like most cafés. Background music coming from the sound system was being played, and positioned centrally on one wall was a wide-screen TV showing a newscaster reading the news, but the volume was muted.

A few tables were strategically dotted about the place, and there was a glass display unit at the back of the shop near the kitchen, showing a selection of foods on offer.

Instead of going to the counter, Aki and Cody

took a seat at one of the tables.

They had a clear view of the room and the people in it, but for some reason, Aki suspected the phone snatchers weren't among the clientele of the café.

A family of six sat at one of the tables and at another table was a young couple, a boy and girl, obviously heavily into one another and on a date.

Cody picked up a menu and began to read as he surreptitiously studied the people in the café.

"Somehow, I don't think any of these people were the ones that mugged you in the park last night. Do you?"

Aki agreed and shook his head. "Wrong ages. And the boy with the girl ... no, I don't think he was with the gang. He also doesn't seem the type to mug someone. He looks like me ... a bit of a geek. So, what's next?"

Before Cody had the chance to answer, a middle-aged woman wearing a navy-blue apron and carrying a notepad and pen came over to their table.

"Hi, have you decided yet? Is there anything on our menu you boys want to try?"

She had a broad Cockney accent and was chewing gum. This was definitely not the type of café Aki would visit with his parents.

"I think we'll order two lattes." Cody looked questioningly across the table at Aki, and Aki nodded his agreement.

"Anything else?" the waitress asked, pen poised. "Something to eat, perhaps?"

"Nothing for me, thanks," Aki said. "But if you happen to have my new iPhone that went missing last night..."

"Excuse me?" The top of the pen the waitress was holding was being repeatedly clicked on and off. "iPhone, did you say?"

Aki looked at Cody with raised brows. He hadn't

expected a response from the waitress. In fact, he'd been sarcastically half jesting when he'd mentioned the phone.

Cody nodded. "Yes, a phone. My friend's phone went missing last night when he was attacked."

"Dexter," the waitress called out over her shoulder in the direction of the café's kitchen. "Come here, now. There are two young gentlemen here that would like a word with you."

From behind a metal-chained curtain that led to the kitchen area, a youth appeared, and in his hand was a cell phone.

Chapter Five

Cody

When Cody walked into the café, he had no idea what he would find. He'd wanted Aki to find his phone but hadn't held out much hope of that happening.

And now, standing in front of them, was one of the youths from last night and he had the evidence in his hand.

"Hand it over," the waitress said.

"Hand what over?" Dexter asked, pretending ignorance. With a flick of his wrist, he swiped his finger across the phone's home page, shutting it down, and then he put it into the back pocket of his tattered denim jeans. His jeans were hanging low on his hips and his hoodie looked like it had seen better days. But although the phone was out of sight it wasn't out of mind.

"Give me that phone. The one you just tried to hide from us," the waitress demanded.

"Mom…" Dexter wailed pathetically.

"Don't Mom me. I'm waiting. Hand it over. These guys would like their property back."

"Huh," Dexter sneered. "Why should I give it back to these pansies?"

Cody watched Aki twist uncomfortably in his seat. His head was down and he looked kind of embarrassed. But Cody wasn't feeling the same way. In fact, he felt the opposite. A rage was building inside him. No one had a right to throw derogatory comments into a conversation like that. Several topics were socially off-limits when it came to aiming insults. Offensive remarks about a woman's body or a person's ethnic background were a no-no. And as for homophobic slurs … it said more about the insecurities of the idiots making those wisecracks than the people they were aimed at.

"What did you say?" the woman asked heatedly. "Did I hear right?"

"Mom, they're queers. Poofters. They deserve to be robbed. I tracked their Google searches and some of the websites they visited. You'll never guess what they were looking at. Dating for gays, homo clubs, that sort of thing."

"Hand over the phone, *now!*"

Cody stood up but it wasn't to stretch his legs. It was to be in a better position if he had to take aim and land a punch. He was never violent, but in this case, he was prepared to make an exception. "I'd like my friend's phone back, please. It won't take two minutes to call the police and report a hate crime. Once they know who's calling, they'll be here in no time."

"And who exactly do you think you are?" Dexter scoffed. "Someone famous?"

Cody felt the firm pressure of Aki's hand on his arm as if Aki was trying to prevent him from attacking Dexter.

"Don't, Cody, it's not worth the trouble," Aki said.

"He's Cody Freeman. The drummer from Trend." But it wasn't Aki that had said those words, it was the youth sitting in the corner of the café with his girlfriend that had spoken.

But that wasn't where all eyes were focused. The glass door to the café had opened and everyone was looking at two guys dressed in black, standing in the doorway, aiming their pistols at Dexter.

"Oh, *shit.* If it isn't Tom and Jerry," Aki murmured under his breath, but it was loud enough for Cody to have heard.

"What the fuck!" Dexter was visibly panicking

and had turned as white as a sheet.

"How did you find me?" Aki asked.

One of the tall, muscular security guards shrugged and holstered his gun. His coworker followed suit.

"It wasn't too difficult. When we realized you had dodged Cassie's eagle eye and left your parents' flat, all our resources went on finding you. Using your iPhone's Global Positioning System, we've been staking this place out since the early hours of the morning. It was only when you came to the café that we discovered the GPS coordinates. Although they were linked to your iPhone, they hadn't been showing us exactly where *you* were. We've been waiting for the all-clear from headquarters before we came in to find you, Your Highness."

"And now that you've found me?"

Cody noticed Aki didn't deny the royalty bit.

"We'll be taking you home ... like ... right now," the bodyguard said.

Had the bodyguard been serious when he had called Aki, Your Highness? Perhaps he was being sarcastic and Aki was just a spoiled brat who had been out on the town, having fun at the expense of others.

Cody stretched out his hand in Dexter's direction. "We're not leaving until my friend has his phone back."

"Don't worry, Cody. I told you, the phone's not that important. I can easily buy another one."

"Then why have we come in search of it?"

Aki sighed. "It's the principle of the thing. If guys like Dexter can get away with beating someone up for an iPhone, or even attacking someone just for fun, then who's going to teach them a lesson?"

The waitress put her hands on her well-proportioned hips and puffed out her ample bosom. "Oh, I'll make darn sure Dexter learns from what he's done. He'll face the consequences, all right. He won't be going out with his friends for at least a couple of months," she said. "As his mother, I'll see he regrets what he's done. It's not the way his father and I raised him or his brothers. We might not have a posh education like some people, but we know right from wrong, and Dexter ought to know he shouldn't have done what he did. And as for calling you both ... um ... names, he'll be sorry for that, too."

Cody took the phone from Dexter and passed it to Aki.

"I think we ought to leave now. Don't you?" Cody asked, and Aki nodded.

Putting a couple of notes under the sugar bowl, Aki said, "For the coffee, and keep the change."

"But you didn't have anything," Dexter's mom said.

"I know, but we placed an order. Some people don't take anything for nothing ... and that's us. Thank you for your time and for returning the phone."

Leaving the café, the long menacing shadows of the bodyguards followed them as the two men walked protectively behind. A black limo was parked across the road and one of the men walked over to the car and opened the door. He waited for Aki to get in, while the other climbed into the driver's seat.

The bodyguards were on pause as Aki said his goodbyes.

"So, I guess this is *adios*," Cody said.

"Looks like it."

Cody felt strange. It was almost as if he was about to lose something precious. It wasn't as if he had built a real friendship with Aki in such a short space of time, but something had happened last night. They had been in a fight together. They had bonded, and now it seemed they were about to go their separate ways.

"Are you really royalty?" Cody asked. He was almost afraid to know the answer. If Aki was a genuine royal, then that would mean they were out of one another's social circles. There would be no way he could have Aki, a *prince*, as a friend. Their lifestyles would be totally different.

"I'm sort of royalty," Aki replied and shrugged as if it were of no importance. "My father's a prince and that makes me a prince too. But I'm only a minor prince. I'm no one special. We are distant relatives to the king."

"But you're special enough to have two bodyguards."

"That's more to do with my father being a billionaire than being a prince."

It was strange having this conversation on the street.

"Do they follow you everywhere?" Cody flicked his gaze to the two men in dark suits.

"Last night was the first time I managed to lose them and look what happened ... I got mugged."

"Yes, but something good came from last night's adventure. We met. And that would never have happened if you hadn't gone out on your own. So that's a positive thing. Don't you agree?"

Aki laughed and nodded. "I guess I'd have to say it was worth being mugged. But what happens now?"

"What do you mean?" Cody asked. "Logically, I suppose you go your way and I go mine. After all, you're a prince. You wouldn't want to hang out with a want-to-be rock star, would you?"

Aki shifted from one foot to the other and was looking everywhere except in Cody's direction. He seemed reluctant to leave. It wasn't just the tall, dark bodyguards lurking close by that made Aki seem vulnerable, it was the way his shoulders were hunched and his hands were thrust deep into his denim pockets. As if he were a little boy lost.

Cody's protective instincts kicked in.

"Look, it's Saturday and you've probably plenty to keep you busy, but if you've nothing better to do, do you want to come along to the band's practice session this afternoon? We're running through a new song before we play it on stage tonight. You can see how we work and maybe get to know us."

"Sure. Great," Aki said eagerly. "Of course, I'd like to see you play. Where do we have to go?"

Cody wasn't sure if he was happy or frightened by the commitment he'd just made. It wasn't every day he asked royalty if they wanted to tag along.

"Well, firstly, because I now know you're not homeless and you actually do have somewhere to live, I suggest we go to your place and get you a change of clothes. It's not that I mind you wearing my things. I don't. But except for your shoes, everything you're wearing is mine and it's all two sizes too large."

Aki looked down at what he had on and laughed.

"Do I look like a rock star?"

"What?"

"Well, if you usually dress like this, perhaps I could pass as a member of your band."

"I doubt it." Smiling, Cody leaned toward Aki and whispered, "Especially with these two guys shadowing you."

****

Having driven through a security barrier of tall, wrought-iron gates, the limousine pulled up at the door of a large townhouse. Cody was looking at something he could only describe as a mini-palace.

The house had a driveway, and in London, where space was at a premium, that was practically unheard of.

"Do you want to wait downstairs while I go up and change?" Aki asked.

Somehow, through the maze of doors and rooms and corridors, they had reached the kitchen. Aki opened a large silver American-style fridge and pulled out a carton of milk. Taking two glasses from a cabinet, he poured out the creamy white liquid and handed a glass to Cody.

"Thanks," Cody said. "I don't mind waiting here, that's if you're not too long. The practice session begins at two o'clock and I promised the guys I'd be there."

The glass of milk was cold to the touch and downing the drink in one go was satisfyingly refreshing.

"Then you'd better come up to my room and help me choose what to wear. I wouldn't want to embarrass you with my lack of dress sense."

Cody wasn't sure about venturing into Aki's bedroom. A bedroom was a private space. An intimate personal area. But having spent last night together in his Kensington flat, he decided it ought to be all right. Nothing awkward could happen. *Could it?*

Aki's bedroom was at the back of the house and apart from noticing all the computerized electrical equipment and the latest high-tech gadgets, Cody also noticed a window that looked out over the garden. Below, through the sprawling leaves of a climbing rose that twisted through a wooden-framed trellis, he thought he caught a glimpse of a hot tub. In that split-second, he wondered what it would be like to indulge in the luxury of sharing a drink and a soak in the tub on a hot summer's evening with Aki.

When Cody had been studying at college, he'd never been one for hanging out and drinking with the guys as most of his friends had done. He'd usually had his nose deep in a study book or he'd been fine-tuning his drum skills. On a few occasions, he had daringly sneaked into a girl's bedroom in the student's dormitory for a snogging session, but he'd never slept over. He didn't know if his excitement on those occasions had been because he was doing something forbidden—like being in the female wing of the college dormitory—or simply because he was exploring the possibility of getting into bed with a girl for the first time. But this felt different. This was Aki's bedroom and it felt special just being there.

Aki grabbed a few clothes from a wardrobe and opening a drawer, he took out a change of underwear.

"I shouldn't be too long," Aki mumbled. "Just give me a minute and I'll be with you. Meanwhile, make yourself at home."

When Aki disappeared into the en suite, Cody was left to twiddle his thumbs, and with nothing to do, he looked around the room.

Aki had said he was studying to be an electrical engineer and it showed. It looked as if every technical gadget on the market was crammed onto a large worktop table that was pushed against one of the bedroom walls. The gadgets themselves were barely recognizable. Nearly everything had been either unscrewed, opened, and dismembered, or they were half-assembled and awaiting the finishing touches so they could be put into action.

But what caught Cody's eye and held his interest were the countless number of small metal electrical plates with fine-wired circuitry welded to shiny silver power points that were scattered anywhere and everywhere across the worktop.

What was Aki trying to create?

Cody zoned in on a microwave that had its cover off and its innards displayed. He reached out to touch it but was stopped by a warning voice behind him.

"I wouldn't if I were you. You could lose your

fingers."

Cody hurriedly pulled back his hand.

"Why? What is it?" he asked.

"Would you believe me if I told you, it's a prototype … a transporter … and that I'm working with NASA on a quantum mechanics project? Maybe someday, if I can get this thing to work, we can be transported from star to star and perhaps even different galaxies."

"Yeh … as if!" Cody laughed. "For now, I'm just aiming to reach stardom here on earth, and if I'm honest, that's like trying to fly to the moon and back."

"Well…" Aki rested a hand on Cody's shoulder and whispered. "If it's any consolation, after saving me from those thugs last night, you'll always be my *superstar*."

Aki had dressed, and in Cody's opinion, he looked sexy. He wasn't muscular like most of Cody's friends, and he wasn't particularly artistic looking, with long hair and clothes to match, like the members of Trend. But Aki had a style all his own. Dressed in tight butt-hugging denim jeans and a cream roll-neck cashmere sweater, and despite his thick-framed geeky glasses, it was a look that Cody could only call "monied chic" and "understated sexy."

Aki looked like a million dollars, and from what he'd let slip about his parents being worth a buck or two, that was probably the price tag on his clothes and the things in his room.

Cody had gained an insight into Aki's world, and he was sure it wasn't a world he could belong to. Millionaire parents, bodyguards, and a lifestyle that spoke of the ability to do whatever he wanted, whenever he wanted, well, that was beyond Cody's realm of normality.

Cody was still struggling to make ends meet, and being a rock star was working for now, but it could all change tomorrow. That was the deal in a celebrity's world. One moment, you were the flavor of the month, and the next, no one knew who you were.

For now, Cody was pursuing his passion and his dreams of being a drummer but he often wondered how long it would last.

Chapter Six

Aki

Entering through a side entrance, Aki was surprised by how dark and dingy the stairwell of the Turnabout Concert Hall in Central London was. From the outside, Turnabout looked like an elegant Georgian building, and it was, or at least the part that paying customers saw seemed painted, polished, and maintained. But backstage, where the artists' dressing rooms were found, and where all the stage props and musicians' gear were kept, it was another story.

Basic wasn't the word. Bare wooden floorboards and naked lights were the norm. But then again, Aki was usually surrounded by over-the-top luxury, so it was a bit of a surprise to see how the other half lived.

Entering the dressing room, Aki was met with a crowd of faces staring at him, all curious to know who he was.

Cody stepped forward. "Hey, guys, let me introduce you to Aki, a friend of mine. I hope there are no objections if he joins us this afternoon. I said he was welcome to come and see what we do during practice. Aki, this is Mitch, Brent, Sam, and Holly, my bandmates, and this is Paul, our boss."

Holly smiled and waved a hand in Aki's direction, and Brent and Sam followed suit, but Aki thought Mitch appeared reluctant to greet him in a positive way.

"Is he one of your followers or is he just a fan of Trend?" Mitch asked. There was the usual sarcastic tone in Mitch's voice, but not having met Mitch before, Aki didn't know that.

Aki didn't want to cause trouble for Cody. "Look, if it isn't convenient for me to be here, I'll split," he offered.

Aki felt the reassuring touch of Cody's hand on his shoulder.

"Come on, Mitch, give a little. Don't be such a prick. Aki's a friend of mine and I'd like it if he got to know everyone and see exactly what we do."

"He'll probably get in the way of us practicing," Mitch protested, gruffly.

It seemed Mitch wasn't going to play ball and not wanting to be the reason for any aggravation, Aki was about to turn around and walk out, but Paul chipped in.

Paul held out his hand toward Aki and said, "Hi, I'm Paul Canton. And any friend of Cody's is welcome here. Isn't that right, guys?" All heads nodded, although Mitch still seemed reluctant to consent. "I'm not sure if Cody's told you, but we're about to have a practice session. The group has a new song they'd like to run through before this evening's performance. If you're up to it, you can come and sit with me in the concert hall and listen to what's going on. They're not too bad, but in my opinion, you can never get enough practice. The more you practice a song, the better you get. Isn't that right, guys?" Again, the group nodded in agreement.

It seemed Paul had a handle on things and could control any tensions brewing, especially with Mitch.

Aki wondered if Mitch was the alpha male of the group—the one that liked to be in control.

Was there some sort of power struggle going on?

Leaving the dressing room in a chaotic mess, the group made their way through the back corridors of the hall until they arrived at the stage. But Aki didn't go on stage. Paul flipped his hand, giving a signal to follow.

"We'll sit in these seats and listen while they play," Paul explained. They moved toward a row of seats to the right of the stage. "You can get a better impression of what they do from here."

Paul eased off his leather jacket and laid it over the back of a seat before claiming another.

There was a relaxed atmosphere as Trend tuned their instruments and got ready to practice. And then came that moment when a hushed silence fell and they were ready to lead into the song.

Paul gave Aki a nudge and whispered, "Wait for it…"

The performance began.

The gentle strokes of Cody's brushes gave a soft muted sound effect as they tapped out a steady rhythm on the taut skin of his drums. As the crescendo built and was joined by Brent's delicate touch on the strings of his acoustic guitar and Sam's on the wires of his electric, the volume and scale of the music grew steadily louder. Holly's percussion bells added depth and then the crowning glory of Mitch's angelic-sounding voice completed the circle adding to a fantastic melody.

Mitch might be a pain in the ass, but there was no denying he had talent as a singer. His voice was pure, clear, and mesmerizing.

When the song came to an end, Aki heard Paul's sigh of relief followed by the words, "Perfect."

Having listened to a great practice session, just when they were about to clap and shout positive feedback to the band members on stage, there came a loud blast from several amplifiers. Pandemonium broke out as flames emerged from one of the sound boxes.

"What the…" Paul said.

Aki watched helplessly as Paul scrambled over the backs of the seats and climbed onto the stage.

Smoke was billowing and the warning alarms in Turnabout Hall were sounding. With the speed of light, Cody came out from behind his drum kit and disappeared off stage only to return with a fire extinguisher clutched in his hands.

Aki's heart pounded frantically in his chest. As flames and smoke danced about the sound box, he was worried for Cody's safety. The thought of Cody being burnt or injured was terrifying.

In a flash, Cody had the fire under control, and with everyone safe and the damage kept to a minimum, they were all able to take a deep breath and relax. The sound of gentle laughter could be heard coming from the band members, but it wasn't the sound of merriment, it was the sound of relief. They were alive and unharmed.

At the back of the concert hall, the double doors were flung open and hit the walls on either side with a loud bang. Four firefighters, dressed in heavy-duty protective gear with oxygen cylinders strapped to their backs, stormed in.

"Where's the fire?" one of the firemen called out.

All four men were walking down the aisle toward the stage.

"Anyone hurt?" called another.

Aki was surprised at how fast the fire service had arrived at the venue once the alarm had been sounded. It turned out the fire engine and crew had been on their way back to the station after dealing with a fire in a different part of the city. When dispatch had radioed the news about a fire at The Turnabout, they had reached the scene in a matter of minutes.

With the all-clear given and the fire crew gone, an eerie hush fell over everyone.

"What do you guys say to having a drink and a pie at the pub across the road to calm our nerves?" Paul ran his hands through his disheveled hair. "The fire was a bit traumatic, or at least it was for me, and I could do with a break. We can come back here later and clear away this mess before tonight's gig."

"Sounds good to me," Brent said.

"As long as you're paying," Mitch added with a laugh.

Paul climbed off the stage and collected his jacket from where he'd left it. "Then a drink it is. Let's go."

And they all followed.

****

When the pub lunch was over, Aki returned to the Turnabout Concert Hall with the others and although he was with the group, he really had eyes only for Cody.

Just looking at Cody, his heart beat faster. Strange feelings of self-consciousness and excitement surged, but he knew he had to keep hold of his passion. He didn't want to be wounded. Still new to this emotion, he wasn't sure if it was purely a physical attraction he was feeling for Cody, or if there could be a chance to build something deeper and more meaningful with him.

Could Cody feel the same tempting fascination he felt? If he invested his time and energy into building a relationship, would it be just his luck that Cody turned out to be straight? He hoped not.

Cody was older than he was. True, only by one year. But he was out in the big wide world fending for himself, whereas Aki was still living a protected life under his parents' roof.

"I suppose we ought to make a start," Holly said. "I'll go and see if I can find a mop and bucket somewhere. The floor will need a good scrub where the smoke has marked the floorboards, but other than that, it shouldn't be too much work to get things ready."

Aki had no idea how he could help, but he was willing to roll up his sleeves and lend a hand. The mess from the fire still had to be cleared but when Brent picked up his guitar and started to play, it looked like the gig might not be happening.

"I can't get any sound from my guitar," Brent moaned. "Not a note."

Cody found a drumstick and hit the drums. "Hey, Brent. I don't think it's your guitar that's not working. I think the whole sound system is kaput. My drums are fine but there's no connection to the amplifiers. Which means we might be able to play, but no one will hear us."

"We're fucked," Mitch said and stormed off to find consolation in smoking a cigarette outside.

Sam walked over to one of the amplifiers and started to turn it, looking for the problem. "Well, I can't see what's wrong with it and I've no idea how to fix it, do you?" He was looking around the remainder of the group.

They all shrugged their shoulders, and then Paul said, "Don't look at me, I'm only the manager. The only thing I know about electronics is that there's usually a plug and a socket involved."

Aki, seeing the panic in everyone's eyes at not being able to play that evening, cautiously raised his hand.

"Um … would anyone mind if I had a look? I mean, just like you guys, I've no idea what's wrong, but I could give it a go and try and repair the amp."

"What makes you think you can fix the equipment?" Paul asked. "I mean … I've no objection to you trying, but why do you think you can?"

"Aki's studying electronic engineering," Cody explained. "He's got this room full of electrical gadgets and all sorts of other things he's working on. And if he says he might be able to fix the amplifiers, then I believe him. At least it's worth a try, don't you think? Anyway, what have we got to lose?"

"Nothing, I guess. Just a couple of thousand pounds worth of equipment, that's all." Paul pointed to the amplifiers. "But hey, feel free to give it a go."

Aki could easily have offered to send one of his bodyguards to a music store to buy new equipment for the group, but he didn't. Instead, he felt up to the challenge of repairing the amplifiers, and rolling up his sleeves, he set to work.

Kneeling beside one of the boxes, he pulled out a small zip case from the pocket of his jeans, and opening it up, he found a screwdriver that suited the size of the screw he was looking at. The tool case was about the size of an iPhone. It didn't take much room and it wasn't heavy to carry around. And he always liked to have a set of tools handy, just in case there were moments like these.

Having smoked his cigarette, Mitch walked back into the concert hall and when he saw what was happening, said, "Who the fuck does he think he is? And why is he tampering with our stuff?"

It was a negative attack and the group looked ruffled by Mitch's comments.

"Hey, cool it, Mitch. Give the kid a chance. He's offered to help and as no one else knows how to fix it, we thought we'd let him have a go."

"Fix what? You mean everything's broken?"

Sam frowned and began to move the guitars to the side of the stage, away from Holly and her mop. "If you had stayed here and not walked off when we were about to start cleaning, you'd know that."

"I'm not the cleaning type. I leave that to the women in my life."

The unexpected reaction to Mitch's glib remark was that Holly thrust the handle of the mop into Mitch's hand.

"Here, you do it. As I'm not one of the women in your life, I see no reason for you not to get stuck in, or are you too stuck up to help?"

Ignoring the heated argument that was gathering momentum, Aki connected a few wires, twisted a few knobs, and *presto*, a noise came from the speakers.

Brent smiled and clapped Cody on the back. "Hey, cool. I guess your friend has a purpose after all. Aren't you glad you brought Aki along with you today?"

Mitch scoffed. "I expect Mr. Geek here has more than one purpose ... especially when it comes to using *screwdrivers*. Isn't that right, *Cody*."

There was a nasty sneering tone in Mitch's voice and Aki could see Cody was on edge.

"Hey, enough of that, Mitch," Brent intervened. "There's no need to get nasty. And besides, Aki has just done us a big favor. He's repaired the amplifiers and we'll be able to play this evening."

"It's not about favors," Cody said. "It's about the way Mitch spoke to my friend that I object to. No one should speak to Aki or any other person like that, and Mitch should be made to realize this."

"Oh, sorry," Mitch said with sarcasm in his voice. It hadn't been a real apology with feeling behind the words. He had been mocking them. "Perhaps I shouldn't have said *geek*. Perhaps I ought to have said *gay*!"

Aki started to collect his gear together. He hated confrontation of any kind, and when he saw Cody restlessly clenching and unclenching his fists, he knew he had to leave before he became the cause of a fight. "It's all right, Cody. Don't worry about it."

"I'm not worried," Cody said between clenched teeth. "I'm fuming. It just shouldn't happen, that's all. He shouldn't have said that to you."

"Why?" Mitch asked. "Are you worried I'll say it to you, Cody?"

"We're out of here," Cody said. "And we won't

be coming back this evening. Come on, Aki, let's go home … now."

When Cody jumped down from the stage and waited for Aki to follow, there was a hushed silence in the group. They obviously hadn't expected Cody to protest and walk out.

Brent stepped toward the edge of the stage. "Hey, man, don't take any notice of Mitch. He doesn't mean it. You know what he's like. He says the most awful things sometimes, but there's usually no harm behind his words."

"Well, it didn't come across like that just now," Cody said. "I didn't like what he said to Aki and I'm not standing for it. And it wasn't just Aki he was rude to. He also had a go at Holly for being a woman. Mitch is sexist, homophobic, and—"

"All right, Cody. We get the message." It was Paul that had spoken. "I agree with you. And as manager of this group, I'm not allowing discrimination of any sort, now or in the future. All are welcome here. If it's legal and the law permits, then it's allowed. End of. And there will be no disrespect shown to anyone. If you can't act with respect to one another, then you're out. Got it?"

The message was coming across loud and clear, and it was obvious by the way Mitch stormed off, that he knew he was the brunt of Paul's lecture.

"Now…" Paul took a deep steadying breath. "Let's all go home, have a shower and a rest, and we'll meet back here at seven for the concert. Are we happy with that?"

Everyone nodded in agreement and went to collect their belongings from the dressing rooms, but when Cody and Aki were about to leave, Paul called them back.

"Look, perhaps I'm overstepping the mark here,

and perhaps I shouldn't say anything and keep my nose out of other people's business, but I think you two should know. I'm sure Mitch didn't mean anything personally when he mentioned gays. It's just that a couple of months ago, something bad happened."

"To Mitch?" Cody asked.

"No, it didn't happen to Mitch, exactly. It happened to his younger brother. Alf was in school—gym class—when he was approached by some boys. They were messing around and it got out of hand. I don't know all the details, but I believe it could have been nasty. Luckily someone raised the alarm before anything bad happened, but it threw Mitch for six. As an older brother, he was always very protective of Alf, and he blames himself for what could have occurred. Mitch now has a downer on boys and men and any sort of relationships between two people of the same sex. I'm assuming that's why he was a bit—"

"Homophobic?" Cody asked.

"That's your word, not mine," Paul said.

"Well, thanks for explaining. It makes things clearer." Aki could now understand why Mitch was the way he was, but it didn't make the stigmatizing and name-calling any easier to bear.

"I trust you'll keep this confidential, but I thought you ought to know where Mitch is coming from. I'm sure he doesn't mean to be nasty to you personally, it's just that…"

"He's hurt," Aki said. "And I understand."

Cody shook his head. "Well, I have to disagree. I understand, and knowing what happened makes things clearer, but it still doesn't give Mitch the right to be rude to Aki … or to anyone else."

"And I agree. And that's why I've come back to apologize in person."

Mitch walked back onto the stage and had been waiting quietly in the wings, listening to Paul's explanation of the situation.

"Sorry, Mitch," Paul said. "If I've said anything I shouldn't have…"

"No, no, no. It's all right." Mitch thrust his hands deep into the pockets of his stylishly torn and tattered denim jeans. "You did what you thought was necessary. And it was necessary. I shouldn't have said what I did, and I apologize to Aki and also to Cody for having caused any offense." Then, just as quietly and unobtrusively as Mitch had returned to the stage, he once again left.

With those few words of regret spoken by Mitch, Aki knew Mitch was genuinely sorry.

"All right then. Time to head home and get some rest before tonight's performance." Paul was trying to sound upbeat as if to lighten the heavy mood of the moment. "Oh, and Aki, we'll expect to see you here tonight. You never know, the amplifiers might explode again and we'll need you to fix them. By the way, how would you like a job for the summer? Cody mentioned your college holidays are starting soon. You're more than welcome to come to Amsterdam with us as our sound technician. The pay won't be that great, but you'll have the chance to see part of Europe for free … although you'll probably have to bunk with Cody."

Aki didn't bother to tell Paul he had already traveled to places Paul could only dream of. There was practically nowhere on the planet he hadn't already visited.

"Thanks, Paul. I'd really love to join you, but I'll have to see if I can squeeze you and Trend into my agenda before I promise anything. I'm kinda busy at the moment." Aki wasn't kidding, although Paul might think he was. Aki had projects to finish before college term ended and then there was NASA waiting in the wings for the prototype of the transporter he was building. But the thought of being with Cody and sharing a room together was more than tempting. "Does Cody know about me coming to Amsterdam? He might object to sharing his room with me."

"It was his idea that I ask you," Paul said. "You must be someone special or at least someone he's taken a shine to because I've never known Cody to ask for a favor before."

Aki's stomach flipped and his heart pounded. Did Cody really want him in Amsterdam?

"Come on," Cody said. "It's time I took you home so you can have a shower before coming back here tonight. You're covered in smoke from the fire."

Aki noticed Cody hadn't denied any of the things Paul had said about being special.

"Home? Is that your place or mine," Aki asked, uncertain.

Cody hesitated. "Which would you prefer?"

Was that an open invitation? Aki wasn't sure.

Aki took a steadying breath and chanced his luck. "What about coming to stay with me for a change? There's plenty of room at the house. We could collect some of your clothes on the way and…"

"And then we wouldn't have to worry about Tom and Jerry sitting outside of my flat in the car all night, scaring the neighbors."

"Sounds good to me." Aki's lips widened into a smile and with a feeling of excitement, he left Turnabout Concert Hall with Cody close by his side.

Aki knew his life was about to change.

Chapter Seven

Cody

Over the next three weeks, Cody and Aki formed an unlikely yet unshakable bond. Cody had made sure all Aki's college projects had been completed, and during that time, they also spent countless hours getting to know one another on a deeper level. As an only child, Cody wasn't used to sharing his time, but with Aki, it was easy. He found himself opening up and sharing a part of himself he'd never shared with anyone else before. Often into the early hours of the morning, they would sit and talk about anything and everything. No subjects were taboo. And it was during one of those intimate evenings that the topic of Aki's sexuality was broached.

"You do realize I'm gay, don't you?" Aki had asked.

Cody couldn't remember what had triggered the conversation … it had just happened.

"Yeah, sure," he said with a nonchalant shrug as if he didn't care. Which wasn't true. He did care, and secretly he was curious. "I thought it was obvious. Anyway, why are you asking? Does being gay bother you?"

Cody had no idea where the conversation was going, but he was willing to find out.

"Most friends I know, and it's not as if I have many, want to know all the gory details. They want to know why I prefer boys to girls and they want to know what it's like to kiss someone, and more often than not, they want to know if I've done it!"

"And what do you tell them?"

"I tell them to mind their own business, of course." Aki lifted his brows and gave a flirty, cheeky laugh.

"Then, I suppose there's no need for me to ask the same questions, is there?"

He hadn't told Aki that he was interested to know what the answers would be on a personal level. Or that he often wondered what it was like for someone to be gay and have feelings for a boy. Or that while thinking about these things, he questioned if he himself was indeed a closet gay, not daring to confess, and was simply waiting for the right partner to come along and stir his senses before he came out.

It was strange, but he felt a closeness to Aki that he'd never experienced with a girl, and his mind and emotions were in turmoil, yet he couldn't speak about it. Not even with Aki. Not until he'd gotten it straight in his head and heart where exactly his true feelings and sexual needs lay.

All Cody knew was that Aki was different. Aki was special, he wasn't intrusive, and Cody liked being with him.

If Cody said he had to practice or work on his music scores, Aki was fine with that. Aki just tended to wander off and tinkle with one of his gadgets, or if they happened to be staying at Cody's flat, then Cody would often look over his shoulder to find Aki on the laptop. He'd be working on equations that looked like a foreign language or FaceTiming with lab technicians in another country. They were together ... a lot ... but they weren't in each other's space or faces.

"Hey, the band's not working tonight." Cody passed Aki a toasted sandwich and took a seat on the futon sofa beside him. "What do you say we hit the town and do something different for a change? It just seems like we're either at your place or we're here, spending time at mine. Don't you want to go out ... together?"

Cody shifted on the lumpy futon, trying to find a more comfortable spot. The futon was the place where Aki crashed when he stayed over. And although Aki sleeping on the sofa wasn't a problem, a dent was beginning to form from Aki's frequent use.

"What do you say to a flick and a burger?" Aki suggested.

"A flick?"

"Yeah. Go to the movies. Take in a film."

"I know what a flick is. I just wondered if you did."

The film they eventually watched had been an intense fast, action-packed thriller. But it wasn't the film that Cody remembered the most, it was the way his body had felt as he sat next to Aki in the darkened cinema.

Leaving the cinema and going in search of the much-needed burger, Cody said, "We'll have to do this again sometime." But there hadn't been another chance.

The following week, they were on a plane, flying to Amsterdam.

****

Before leaving England, Cody had taken Paul to one side and explained about Aki being Asian royalty and the need for two bodyguards to lurk in the background. Paul had said it wasn't a problem, as long as they didn't get in the way of Trend's performances, and they didn't.

At first, Tom and Jerry, whose real names were Ron and Jim, stuck out like sore thumbs, but having gotten rid of the black suits and dark sunglasses in favor of worn jeans and faded t-shirts, they managed to blend into the background without too much trouble.

The group had signed a month's contract, and it was a week since they had started playing in Amsterdam, and everything was going great. The members of Trend were staying in a boutique hotel on the Herengracht which was only a short walk to the venue where they played to a full house every night.

The fans seemed happy, but most of all, Cody was happy. His friendship with Aki was growing and they shared a closeness that wasn't there with the other members.

"You know, Cody, I think I need to thank you," Aki said. He had made a pot of coffee and he set a steaming cup of the hot liquid down on the writing desk in front of Cody.

Their hotel room, although stylish, was shabby-chic and in some respects sort of basic. According to Paul, it was all Trend's budget could afford, and they had to like it or leave it. Cody and Aki's room had two single beds, a writing desk, and a chest of drawers on which a service tray had been placed. On the tray was a red electric kettle and various things for making a hot drink of tea or coffee. Cody wasn't sure how luxurious the other band members' rooms were but it didn't really matter. He was happy with what he and Aki had.

"Thank me? Why?" Cody scrolled down on the web page he was searching. He was looking for ideas. He wanted to buy a small gift, a souvenir, and have it sent to his parents in England. It had to be something special.

"You've given me breathing space." Aki slumped down on one of the beds. "Seeing you look for something to take home for your mom and dad has made me realize just how close you are to your parents and just how distant I am from mine."

"But I'm sure your parents love you."

"I'd like to think they do, but sometimes I have my doubts. Especially now. When I told them I was coming to Amsterdam with you, they more or less said, 'fine', and no questions were asked. They didn't even want to know your name. I think they assumed you were a friend from college and you would have already been vetted and cleared by the teachers."

"What do you mean ... vetted?"

"Well, as I've told you, the college I go to is full of rich kids ... and I mean rich. Filthy rich. If the college has already checked your credentials and you are good enough to study there, then my parents wouldn't have worried about who you are. And they didn't. They just said 'fine', and allowed me to come to Amsterdam with you."

"But if I was the wrong type for you to mix with then surely Ron or Jim or one of your other bodyguards would have told them."

"Possibly. I don't really know. Perhaps I'm just put out about how good your relationship is with your parents. Maybe I'm just envious."

Seeing how miserable Aki looked, Cody stood up from the desk and walked over to sit next to him on the bed. He wasn't touching Aki, but he could feel his body heat.

"Look, instead of me finding something online to send to my parents, what do you say to us hitting the streets and the shops together? You might discover something your mom and dad would like to have and we could buy it for them."

"You're such a good friend to me, Cody. Why hadn't we met sooner?"

Cody draped an arm around Aki's shoulder and gave him a hug. It was a hug that could have so easily turned into something more, but at that moment, there was a knock on the bedroom door.

"Just making sure everything's as it should be." It was Ron doing the afternoon security check. Since Aki's adventure into the nightlife of Hyde Park, security around him had been tightened. Every four hours there was a point of contact made between Aki and the bodyguards. Cody had even become used to the bedroom door being opened at two and six o'clock in the morning. Someone always looked in to see if Aki was still in his bed, and then discreetly closed the door.

"We're doing all right, thanks, Ron," Cody said. "But just to let you know, Aki and I will be going out shortly. We're heading for the Kalverstraat. We've been looking online and we've seen some good shops we'd like to visit. We shouldn't be too long getting the things we need, and we'll be back in time for this evening's performance. You don't need to worry about us."

Ron's face cracked with a grin and he shook his head. "Oh, I won't be worrying and neither will Tim. We'll be with you and Aki every step of the way."

"Oh no..." Aki moaned. "There goes our afternoon of enjoyment."

To be fair, Cody thought Ron and Tim had always maintained a discreet distance and respected Aki's privacy. But this outing was supposed to be something only he and Aki enjoyed. It obviously wasn't to be.

"Ron's right," Cody said. "If anything happened to you, he and Tim would be hammered. From what you've told me about your parents, I wouldn't put it past them to make mincemeat of us all. They'd have my head severed from my neck, and I'd hate to think what they'd do to your bodyguards."

From the doorway, Ron nodded and winked in agreement. He then disappeared.

"I suppose I'll have to bite the bullet and take the pain with the gain," Aki said and frowned, but there was a half-smile on his lips as if he was trying not to laugh. "At least I'll have you all to myself this afternoon and Trend and your fans can have you this evening."

Cody collected their jackets from the closet and

walked to the door.

"Then it's a deal, come on. Let's see what the city of *sex and drugs and rock and roll* has to offer us."

****

That afternoon was really the first time Cody and Aki had ventured out to explore what Amsterdam had to offer. After their gig was over, Trend, *en masse*, had usually gone to a shawarma bar or a brown café to unwind. Exploring the interwoven streets of the city with its canals and bridges had yet to be done.

Cody was looking at the map of the city the hotel had provided. "Are we catching the tram or are we going on foot? It shouldn't be too far to walk. The Palace on Dam Square is almost opposite the Kalverstraat."

Aki groaned. "How about grabbing a cab?"

"You know, I've never known anyone like you for taking the easy option. What's wrong with a bit of exercise? You'll be saving the planet, saving gas, and stretching your muscles at the same time."

"Actually, I was thinking of you when I suggested taking a cab. You'll be on stage all night and I wouldn't want to tire you out before your performance."

"I've got plenty of energy for walking and also for the gig tonight. And more than likely, I'll have loads left over for whatever's thrown at me afterward."

"Such as?" Aki asked

Cody thought he heard a hint of flirtation in Aki's voice. Was Aki coming on to him or was he receiving mixed messages?

It was good to have Aki all to himself and to be out in the city, away from the other members of Trend. Shopping or visiting a mall wasn't usually his sort of thing, but it gave them something to do and got them away from the confines of the enclosed hotel room.

As the afternoon progressed, Cody enjoyed

playing the tourist and he guessed by the smile on Aki's face and the relaxed way he was walking beside him, that Aki did too.

Reaching Dam Square, they took photos of the ancient façade of the Palace and then watched the unruly, squabbling pigeons as they picked at the offering of crumbs and seeds a group of people was tossing in their direction. Having listened to the music of the buskers and licking the rainbow-colored sprinkles from an ice cream they had just bought, they wandered into a side street packed shoulder to shoulder on either side of the street with shops. It was the Kalverstraat.

Most of the shops catered to tourists and they were just what Cody was looking for.

One shop's window was full of brightly-colored knickknacks and having explored what was on offer, Cody nudged Aki and said, "Do you feel like having a look inside?"

Opening the door, they walked into the shop and after about fifteen minutes, came out carrying a couple of bags with presents.

"Not bad for an afternoon's work," Aki smiled. "What's next?"

Cody thought Aki looked really happy. For the remainder of the afternoon, as they sat at sidewalk cafe tables drinking hot chocolate and eating waffles, they had fun. And the trip on a canal barge wasn't too bad either.

"Perhaps when the gig in Amsterdam is over, we can visit another European city during your holiday break. You know, just you and me. What do you say to that?"

"Sounds like a great idea."

As they passed Madame Tussauds on Dam Square, Cody and Aki looked at one another, grinned, and nodded. No words were needed. They just ducked inside the building leaving Ron and Jim standing on the corner of Dam Square wondering where they had gone.

With their tickets bought, Cody and Aki joined a small group making their way into the exhibition. Walking at a steady pace, they passed through various zones showing personalities from the sporting and cinema worlds, but moving on, when they arrived at the display of royalty, Cody felt the urge to tease Aki.

"Well, if I'm honest, I can't see the resemblance between you and these royals. Are you sure you're a prince with royal blood in your veins?"

Aki shrugged. "I might not have their fair skin or a straight nose, but I've been told I'm very hot-blooded."

Cody laughed. "I didn't say hot-blooded, I said royal blood. And besides, I love your aquiline-shaped nose."

Cody reached out and carefully ran his finger along the hooked ridge of Aki's nose. But he hadn't expected Aki's reaction.

They were alone in the zone where the royals were displayed, and with a gentle shove, Aki pushed Cody over to a pillar in the corner. The lights and security cameras were pointed at the exhibits which meant under cover of the darkened room, Cody and Aki were practically hidden from view.

With a gentle thrust, Aki pressed Cody against the pillar, and held there by Aki's negligible body weight, Cody was surprised at how excited he was feeling.

"I didn't say royal," Aki whispered. "I said hot-blooded. Would you like me to show you just how hot I can be?"

Aki didn't wait for a reply. All Cody felt was the scorching heat of Aki's lips as they pressed against his. The kiss wasn't rough and brutal, it was soft and tender, and as Aki's arms crept around Cody's waist, he stiffened, but then he relaxed into it.

The kiss deepened and when Aki's tongue probed and explored, Cody parted his lips and let Aki in.

A soft groan of desire escaped from between Aki's lips.

"Cody, are you all right with this?" Aki asked. "I mean, have you ever kissed a boy before?"

Cody hadn't. And he wasn't about to reveal to Aki that he was a virgin when it came to kissing boys.

"We ought to go," Cody said. "If we stay here much longer, Ron and Tim are bound to come looking for us."

"I suppose you're right," Aki said and sighed. "Perhaps we ought to leave."

"But not before this…" And daringly Cody leaned toward Aki and kissed him hard on the mouth. Aki was left with no doubt that Cody had wanted to kiss him.

Not finishing the tour of Madame Tussauds, Cody and Aki left the building and burst out into the brightness of Amsterdam's strong afternoon sunshine. Cody felt as if he was being reborn. He was a different person from the one that had gone into the building, and he knew he would be forever changed. After kissing Aki, nothing would or could ever be the same again. Cody wanted to capture the moment. It was a moment of freedom, of truly recognizing and becoming himself. He was who he was—he was gay—and he was unashamedly proud of it.

"A photo. We have to take a selfie."

Happy and laughing, Cody grabbed his phone from his back pocket and took a photo of them both. It was a good likeness. Aki looked like his usual self which was beautifully handsome, and although Cody's hair was a mess, he didn't delete the photo. It was a memory. A memory of his afternoon with Aki and a memory of their first kiss.

No ... he wasn't about to delete something so precious.

Defiantly bold and blatantly obvious, Cody and Aki walked back to the hotel hand in hand. It was Amsterdam, the place where almost anything was permitted. It was a free city where your sexuality wasn't questioned. You were just accepted for who you were and what you believed in. And at that moment, Cody believed in a future with Aki. They were heading back to their room at the hotel, together ... and anything could happen.

Chapter Eight

Aki

Aki sensed something was wrong the moment he walked into the lobby of the hotel. Not only were Ron and Tim standing there on the lookout for him, but there were also four other bodyguards waiting—his parents' bodyguards.

"Where are they?" he asked. He wasn't speaking to anyone in particular, he had just thrown the question out there in the hope of getting a quick answer.

"They are waiting for you in the lounge, Your Highness," Ron said.

Aki knew trouble lay ahead. He had gone from being simply "Aki" to being "Your Highness" once again. With the arrival of his parents, a regime of rigid protocol was back in place.

The lounge was to the right of the reception. It wasn't a massive room, but Aki was sure his parents and their entourage had taken over the place. *So much for keeping a low profile,* he thought.

Now everyone would know, even the band members of Trend, that he was in fact a royal prince and not just a kid who was handy with a screwdriver and could fix amplifiers when needed. His cover was blown.

Squaring his shoulders back, Aki made a move toward the lounge but was held back by Cody's hand on his arm.

"Wait," Cody said. "We're in this together. You and me. If you're going to get a verbal thrashing from your parents, then so am I."

"That's kind of you, Cody. But you don't know what you're letting yourself in for."

"Then I'll soon find out, won't I?"

Together they walked into the lounge and Aki saw Cody stiffen and then shock appeared on his face. He could see why. His parents were sitting as if they were holding court.

Two military guards were positioned inside the doorway and another two were stationed beside the French patio doors that led onto the terrace and into the enclosed gardens of the hotel.

"Father, Mother." Aki stepped forward and bowed low over his father's outstretched hand before planting a kiss on his mother's cheek. "You shouldn't have come here. If you had needed to see me, a call could have been made and I would have come home like the obedient son I am."

He was tempted to ask them which of their many homes that would be, but he knew sarcasm would get him nowhere.

"We heard rumors of you being away from your studies ... having fun," his father, Prince Veer, said.

"Then rumors are wrong. All my college projects have been completed and handed in for my tutors to assess. Cody made sure of that."

"Cody?"

"Yes, Cody Freeman, my friend." Aki turned and looked at Cody, and simply smiled.

He had wanted to say *boyfriend* but resisted. He was sure his parents weren't ready to hear those words just yet. He suspected they had no idea he was gay.

Aki watched as Cody stepped forward and gave an awkward bow in the direction of his parents.

"Cody is an even harder taskmaster than you are, Father. He told me if my projects weren't completed, I would have to stay in England and miss out on the trip to Amsterdam."

"And NASA? What has happened to that

project?"

Aki took a deep calming breath. His father had hardly acknowledged Cody. There had only been a slight wave and a flick of the wrist.

"Have no fear, that too will be completed … eventually."

"Eventually?" Prince Veer raised his eyebrows questioningly.

"There are some things you don't rush," Aki said. "And creating a transporter is one of them. At the moment, I have other priorities."

Aki knew his father couldn't question him further about NASA. The project was classified. And he knew his father had no knowledge of how electronics worked, so for once, Aki felt he had the upper hand in the conversation.

"I will accept the fact you believe there is no rush to get to NASA, but I must tell you there *is* a rush to get to Schiphol Airport. Our plane is being refueled and the pilot is waiting on standby for us. You had better hurry and pack your things."

"But Father…" Aki was about to protest, but he stopped. His mother hadn't said a word, but the frown on his father's face spoke volumes. "Yes, sir," he replied and left it at that.

With rage, anger, and frustration building inside him, he turned, and brushing carelessly past Cody, he left the room. He knew there would be no reasoning with his parents at this moment. It would take time and persuasion to make them see how happy he was just being with Cody. For once, he felt valued as a person, as an individual, and as a friend, and he didn't want to lose that.

Swiping the card key on the room door, the lock unclicked and opened, and turning the handle, he entered.

His room—*their* room—was just as they had left it that morning. A shirt Cody had changed his mind about wearing lay crumpled and creased where it had been haphazardly tossed across the back of a chair, and scattered on the floor, near the bottom of his bed were the sneakers he'd forgotten to tidy away. Dirty coffee cups that still needed to be cleaned were on the writing desk, and Aki felt close to tears.

This room was where he and Cody had slept together. Where they had laughed together. And where he had gradually fallen in love with Cody. Sure, Cody was sexy to look at, but his feelings for Cody went deeper. From the start, he'd fancied Cody, but that desire and their friendship had turned into more as his love grew.

Behind him, Aki heard the soft click of the latch as the door was opened and closed. He turned and Cody was there with his arms open wide.

"Come here," Cody said.

That was all the encouragement Aki needed to hear. With eager steps, he walked into the safe haven of Cody's embrace and was held close. He knew he was where he wanted to be. He wanted to be held tightly and forever in Cody's arms.

Aki pressed his head against Cody's chest and allowed the tears to fall.

"I don't want to go. I don't want to leave you," he said.

Cody made him feel so safe, so secure, so protected. He'd never felt like this with anyone else before. If only every day could be like today. No worries. No cares. And no parents breathing down his neck, making him do things he didn't want to do.

Cody's finger went beneath Aki's chin. His face was tilted upward, and Cody's blue eyes showed concern as their gaze met.

"You know you have to go with them, don't you?" Cody said. "You can't stay here, not now."

"I don't see why not."

"Well, one of the reasons you can't stay with me is that after you left the hotel lounge, your father threw an accusation in my face … and I don't want to go to jail."

"Why would you go to jail?"

"He's forbidden me to see you. He says you're still a minor and he's accusing me of kidnapping you."

"I'm eighteen, or almost eighteen. Next month it's my birthday."

"But next month is too late. I might be in prison by then."

Aki stormed to the closet and flung open the door. He pulled out his backpack and with erratic energy, he began stuffing anything and everything he could find into it.

"Damn things, damn life, damn—"

"Hey, cool down," Cody said. "It's only a setback. We can still be friends. It's just that we might have to wait a few weeks before that can happen."

"I don't want to be friends." Aki ran his hands through his hair in frustration. Wasn't Cody listening to what he was saying? "I want to be more than friends with you. Don't you get it? I want a relationship. A proper relationship. A boyfriend-boyfriend relationship. You, me, us … together."

"Look, perhaps it's best if we go our separate ways for now. When you've done your thing and finished your project for NASA and I've completed the tour with Trend, I'll come and find you. When I'm back in England, we can get together and—"

"But I'll lose you. You'll find someone new. You've loads of fans wanting to get to you and—"

"You're worrying about something that's not

likely to happen. I'm not going anywhere." Cody shrugged and a smile tugged at the corners of his mouth. "Well, actually, I am. There's my commitment to Trend. In an hour, I have to meet the guys and get ready for tonight's gig, but other than that, I'm all yours."

Aki realized Cody was trying to inject humor into the moment, but it wasn't really easing his hurt.

"You mean, I'll get to see you again?" Aki asked.

Cody nodded. "When I'm done here, and the group's contract in Amsterdam is over, I'll come and find you."

Was Cody offering a glimmer of hope?

"You promise?" Aki asked.

"I promise."

Aki threw the jeans he was holding down onto the bed and walked unwaveringly over to Cody. His fists bunched as he grabbed hold of Cody's blue striped shirt. Pulling Cody roughly toward him, Aki whispered softly, "Cody, I need a kiss. A proper kiss. If I'm taking the risk of losing you, I need something to remember you by. Something that will keep me going for the next couple of weeks while you're on tour figuring out what you want from me."

And as Cody's lips met his, Aki got what he needed.

****

A week ago, when Aki and his family and their entourage landed in England, he had thought London seemed dark and dismal after the excitement of Amsterdam. In Amsterdam, life and living were cleaner, happier, and more fun. But then of course Cody had been there.

Cody had changed his outlook on life. He now had something to look forward to, and that something was seeing Cody again, sometime soon.

"What has happened to your friend? The one that was playing in that group," his mother, Princess Saura, asked. She circled her hand in the air as if by doing so, she could conjure up Cody's name and what he was doing. "You know, the one that was with you in Amsterdam. The Dutch boy."

Aki's parents had decided to spend some time at their house in London, and while Prince Veer was in the city doing business with his banker, Aki and Princess Saura, and his older brother, Prince Bayani, were in the kitchen sharing lunch.

"Cody isn't from Amsterdam, Mother, and he certainly isn't Dutch. He's just working there for a couple of weeks. He'll be back in England soon."

"Oh, he was working there, was he? But that doesn't answer my question. What has happened to him? Are you still seeing him?"

"I wish I was." Aki sighed and shove the food around his plate. It wasn't that the food was inedible or tasteless, it was just that he wasn't hungry. "He's busy, Mama. And I have no idea when I'll see him next."

"Hey, what's up?" Prince Bayani asked. "You seem a bit down."

Bayani was the firstborn, the golden boy of the family. And although Aki wasn't jealous of his older brother, he did envy his independence. Through no fault of his own, Aki felt he was limited to the confines of the house and his private school education, whereas Bayani, who was five years older, had claimed the chance of freedom from his parents by living and working in New York.

"It sucks being a royal prince," Aki said. "I can't go anywhere or do anything without being monitored. And although Ron and Tim are great guys, it becomes a bit of a bore when you have to have them at your heels

24/7."

Bayani grinned. "I've been there, done that, and got the sticker. You get used to it, you know that. It isn't our fault that our father has billions and is a security risk. We've lived with that problem long enough to be able to cope with it. So, what's really bothering you? What's getting you down?"

"Boredom, loneliness ... everything."

"You mean being away from this musician, Cody?"

"Yes. That's it exactly. It's Sunday, and everyone has a day off on Sunday. We ought to be chilling with friends or family. We ought to be having fun *together*. But instead, I'm stuck here alone."

Aki walked to the French windows that led out to the garden. He stood staring out into nothingness, longing to feel the warmth of Cody's arms holding him and the passion of Cody's lips as they pressed against his.

"What can we do for you, my darling?" his mother asked.

"Nothing, Mama. There is nothing either of you can do."

Aki didn't see it coming. But before he could take action and avoid the onslaught, in one fell swoop, Bayani had lifted him high into his arms and had carried him laughing and kicking in protest, to the pool in the garden.

"Drown your sorrows, my darling brother. And I suggest you find a new interest."

Bayani then unceremoniously tossed Aki into the water fully clothed, but not before Aki had managed to hook an arm around Bayani's leg and pull him into the pool with him.

"Where are my glasses?" Aki asked, frantically looking around for the missing object. Then, seeing his glasses lying at the bottom of the pool, he dove deep to retrieve them.

It was a good half-hour before the brothers called it quits and exited the water. They were exhausted and panting for breath. Still wiping the wet from their faces with their hands and wringing as much moisture from their clothes as they could, Aki and Bayani were about to enter the kitchen when their mother called out, reprimanding them.

"Don't you dare come in here like that, you awful boys!" She laughed. "Think of what Cassie will say if she finds her polished kitchen floor covered with pool water. Strip off and go upstairs and dry yourselves before you make more of a mess."

Obedient to the tone in their mother's voice, they stripped down to their underwear.

Standing on the terrace patio, Bayani wrapped a brotherly arm around Aki and hugged him.

"You're a skinny little urchin, aren't you?" Bayani teased. "You ought to have more meat on you. No wonder you're finding it hard to find a … um … *dating partner*."

Aki hadn't spoken to Bayani about being gay and his preference for boys and not girls, but he was pretty sure his brother had guessed which way his feelings and emotions leaned when it came to that subject.

"Don't walk through the house dripping water everywhere," their mother warned. "Go around to the front of the house and up the stairs that way. If your father were to see you…"

Braving the gravel on the driveway, Aki and Bayani made it unscathed to the front door of the house and knocked. It was Tim who let them in.

Laughing with Bayani at their foolhardiness, Aki was about to climb the grand staircase to his bedroom upstairs but he stopped. His dry clothes were in his room and he needed to get dressed, but out of the corner of his eye, he spotted a white bag on the hall table.

There could be no mistaking the logo on the bag. It was the same bag that had come from the souvenir gift shop in Amsterdam.

"Where did that come from?" Aki asked, pointing to the bag. He felt as if all his energy was draining away from him.

"It was Mr. Freeman, Your Highness. Cody. He was here a short while ago and said you had forgotten to take it with you. He asked if he could leave the bag and told me to pass it to you at a convenient moment."

"Cody was here?"

"Yes, sir."

"But he wouldn't stay?"

Aki didn't understand why Cody hadn't wanted to see him.

"Well, I'm not quite sure." Tim pointed to the library. The doors to the library were open with a clear view of the garden and pool area. "You see, I think he saw the two of you in the pool and thought…"

"Yes?" Aki prompted, wanting to know more. He felt the sharp edge of panic surfacing.

"Well, I'm not sure exactly what he thought. I guess he thought you were having fun and he didn't want to disturb you. And then when you stripped off…"

Aki waited expectantly to hear more, but all Tim did was shrug. Tim didn't have the answers Aki wanted to hear.

Aki turned to Bayani. "I have to go after him. I must find him and explain. Will you come with me?"

But it wasn't Bayani that answered. It was Tim.

"I don't think you should do that. It won't help your situation. Cody said he was on a flying visit from Amsterdam and mentioned something about a change of plans. Instead of staying in London, he said he was going to see his parents and spend the evening with them."

Aki was having difficulty taking it all in. Cody was supposed to be in Amsterdam until the end of the month.

"If I'm honest,"—Tim scratched his head—"I'd say he came to London to spend the day with you and when he got here, what he saw was you and Prince Bayani in the garden. I think Cody got the wrong end of the stick. I don't think he's aware you are brothers."

Now more than ever Aki had to reach Cody and explain. He had to tell Cody that they had to give their relationship a chance and that finding love together was worth fighting for. But had Cody walked away from him forever?

Chapter Nine

Cody

Sunday, there had been no gig scheduled in Amsterdam. The band had a night off, and as they weren't playing until Monday evening, Cody had phoned the airport and booked a cheap flight from Amsterdam to England. It had been a spontaneous impulsive gesture he now wished he hadn't made.

He'd thought if he went to London and saw Aki, even if it was only for one night, the restless sense of longing he felt would ease. But it hadn't. Instead of falling into Aki's welcoming arms, he had been met by the sight of Aki laughing and hugging some unknown stranger. Aki was having fun … and he wasn't.

After leaving Aki's place, Cody had taken a cab to his parents' home which was on the outskirts of London. His unexpected appearance had put his mom in a bit of a panic, but his dad had just opened the door wide and invited Cody to join him in the TV room to watch the second half of a football match. His dad was really laid-back about him being there, but his mom started fussing, wanting to know why his hair had grown so long since he'd been away and why the sudden change in plans.

With the football match ended, they were sitting at the dining room table having a meal.

"Why are you back in London so soon?" his mother asked. "I thought you were away for another week or two?"

"I am," He scooped a few roast potatoes onto a serving spoon and set them on his plate. "I mean, the band is still playing in Amsterdam, but I thought I'd visit a friend in London while I had the chance."

"Some more gravy?" his father asked, holding the

gravy boat over his food.

Cody had a forkful of beef in his mouth so he shook his head, refusing.

His mother pushed the serving dish with the vegetables toward him. "Some more peas, then?" she offered.

Cody swallowed his food. "No, Mom, thanks. It's all right. What's on my plate is fine. I don't need a big meal. In fact, I'm not really hungry."

He had the urge to leave the table and retreat to the safety of his old bedroom. When he'd left Aki's home, he'd had the need to find somewhere private. Somewhere he could lick his wounds and think about what he had to do next.

Instinctively, he had gone to be with his parents. And it was always the same. Whenever anything went wrong, or he was unsure what he should do, he tended to gravitate toward his parents' suburban home where he received unconditional love, because in the past, they were the ones that made everything right again. But this time, they couldn't put a Band-Aid on his hurt or kiss him better. This time, he had to deal with his own emotional scars.

His mother laid down her cutlery and reached across the table and touched Cody's hand. He felt her love.

"What is it, Cody? What's wrong?" she asked.

For a moment, he hesitated, and then he made the decision. He had to tell them. He needed to share what was happening in his life. He wasn't sure how he felt about the changes in his own identity or what he was going to do, but he knew he had to tell them about Aki.

"I've met someone," he said. "And I thought it was serious, but…"

"But?" his mother asked.

"I went to his house and he was there with someone else."

"*He*?" his father questioned with a raised eyebrow.

"Yes, *he*." Cody took a steadying breath and waited for their reaction.

He wasn't sure if his parents would explode and hit the roof with rage or if they would just sit in silence and disbelief not knowing how to react.

His mother stood and came toward him. Her hand rested on his shoulder and she pulled him gently against her side. "Darling, we sort of suspected. Your father and I … well, we've always wondered."

Cody was curious. "How long have you known?"

"As I said, we haven't always known for certain, but when you were eight, I came to your school to collect you. You'd had a swimming lesson, and Jenny Hill, a girl in your class, kissed you outside the swimming baths and—"

"I know. I can remember that kiss. It was the middle of winter. I was standing at the door to the swimming baths and I was freezing. I'd been waiting for you for ages. Snow was on the ground, my hair was wet, and I must have left my coat somewhere inside or on the school bus because I was only wearing my school uniform."

"That coat was expensive. When I told your dad, he was quite cross because you'd lost it, and—"

Cody remembered the moment as if it were yesterday. "She kissed me because I had won the gold badge for being the best swimmer, and she said she loved me. But we were only kids. You couldn't have known I didn't like girls … I mean, not like them in a sexual way."

"Yes, I know. But it was the way you rubbed that

kiss off your face with the back of your hand that said it all. You did it with such disgust and vigor … and you were only eight."

"But even I didn't know I preferred boys. It wasn't until I met Aki that … well, I sort of developed strong feelings for him, and then I realized I'd been pretending to like girls for years."

"Isn't there a chance you could be wrong about your feelings for this Aki person?" his mother asked. "Perhaps you've made a mistake? Perhaps he wasn't with another guy?"

"No, Mom, I'm sure about my feelings for Aki, or at least I was. And I saw him. There was no mistake. He was with another guy messing around in the swimming pool."

Unexpectedly, Cody's father shifted in his seat. "If he's fooling around with someone else, then perhaps he's not the right person for you, son. You have to be serious about a relationship, and if he isn't, then perhaps you ought to move on and find someone new. Like now, before you get hurt."

"Yeah, sure, I suppose you're both right. In fact, I know you are."

But deep down, Cody knew that if he walked away from Aki, he would be letting go of something precious. Something he wasn't likely to find with someone else, anytime soon.

****

It was with a sense of relief that Cody booked a flight to Schiphol and made his way to the airport. He was leaving London, leaving everything familiar to him, and he was leaving Aki behind.

Cody had thought about staying at his flat overnight but decided it would be too depressing. Too painful. He would be remembering Aki, and for now, he wanted to banish Aki from his thoughts.

Seeing Aki with a stranger in the swimming pool had wounded his pride. He had trusted Aki with his feelings, he had shown himself to be vulnerable, and now he felt betrayed.

On the plane, heading back to Amsterdam, he wondered if Aki had found the bag with the souvenirs in it and was now laughing at him. Cody was squirming inside with mortification. He was worried Aki would think he had been too possessively persistent in chasing after him, a royal prince, but that couldn't be helped.

What was done was done. He had been a fool in thinking Aki could return his love, and he had to now accept the fact that Aki had found someone new, and move on.

Arriving at the hotel, Cody paid off the cab driver, and hitching the heavy weight of his backpack onto his shoulder, he walked into the lobby. Apart from the porter and the receptionist, there were a few people around, but it was to Mitch and Brent that his eyes were drawn. They were near the elevators, impatiently pressing the call buttons as if they were in a hurry to get to their hotel rooms.

Cody swapped the weight of his backpack over to his other shoulder and walked with steady steps toward the elevators. As he got there, one of the elevator doors slid silently open, and they all stepped inside.

"What's the hurry?" Cody asked.

"Paul," Brent replied. "He wants to talk over something concerning next week. He's asked us, the group, to meet him in his suite, so we're heading there now. Didn't you get the text?"

Cody shook his head. "I haven't had a chance to look. I've just landed. And my backpack was in the trunk of the taxi and my phone was in my backpack. Actually, it still is. Stupid, I know, but…"

"Landed?" Brent asked.

"Yes, at Schiphol. This afternoon I was in London. I went to see—"

"Don't tell us." Mitch held up his hands, using a gesture traffic cops used when stopping traffic. "Let me guess. You went to see the boyfriend."

Cody couldn't tell if Mitch was being sarcastic or not.

The elevator glided to a smooth halt and they stepped into the dimly lit corridor that led to their rooms. Cody decided he had to face his fears. It was the wrong place and the wrong time, but he might as well get it over and done with, and the sooner the better.

He had already talked about it with his parents, but at some point he would have to tell the world he was gay and he decided he might as well start now. He couldn't go on pretending he was straight forever. He needed to be true to himself and he had to face the consequences.

"Actually, yes. I did go to see my *boyfriend.* Any objections?"

It was irrelevant that Aki had been with someone else and their relationship was now over. His purpose for going to England had been to see Aki. He had thought they were a couple and he couldn't lie about that, not even to Mitch.

Cody could feel his legs shaking nervously and he wondered if they were about to buckle beneath him. What had he done? Having come out as gay, had he just made the biggest mistake of his career?

His stomach flipped and it felt like it had fallen into his boots. He didn't want a confrontation with Mitch, but if that was about to happen, then bring it on.

With toes curled and fists clenched in trepidation,

Cody waited for an onslaught of verbal slurs to be thrown at him. He expected a tirade of laughter. He anticipated the mocking insults of *gay boy*, *fag*, *cocksucker*, and all the other name-calling he had heard before … but they didn't come.

Mitch shrugged his shoulders. "Hey, look, Cody. I'm sorry about what happened before. I really meant it when I apologized. If I was off the mark about you and your boyfriend, I was at fault and I shouldn't have been such a jerk. If you guys have something going, that's all right with me. Go do your own thing."

Mitch, who Cody thought was the one person that would cause trouble, had been the first person to accept him as being gay. Perhaps life wasn't going to be too bad after all.

But when it came to Aki, Cody realized perhaps it was best if he thought of that relationship as being over. He had to think of Aki as someone he had once known.

When he'd met Aki's parents at the hotel, he'd been completely overwhelmed by everything. The security guards, the subtle threats from Aki's father, and then there was the basic fact that Aki was socially out of his league.

Cody wasn't a snob, but when it came to wealth, if he compared Aki's home to his parents' suburban semi-detached, his mom and dad's house could almost fit into Prince Veer's garage.

So, no! He'd thought about it and came to the decision that a relationship with Aki wasn't doable. In fact, realistically, it never had been. Thinking with his head and not his heart, he knew he should avoid Aki like the plague but he wasn't sure he was strong enough to do so.

A noise came from his backpack. His mobile phone was ringing and he guessed it was Aki, trying to get in touch, but he had to stay strong and ignore him.

It was time to move on with his life and forget this newfound feeling of love. He had to forget Aki.

Chapter Ten

Aki

Aki had dressed. His dark hair was damp from the shower, and wearing beige-colored chinos and a black turtleneck sweater, he looked sleek and sharp.

Entering the kitchen, his mother was still sitting at the table where he'd left her. The remains of lunch had been cleared and taking the place of plates and wineglasses was her laptop. She was revamping her website.

Not only was Aki's father heavily into banking and global investment trading, but his mother also had her own interests. She marketed jewelry for designer friends and planned events such as art fairs or online bargain parties, which she never attended. She claimed to be always too busy.

"Has Bayani come downstairs yet?" Aki asked with annoyance.

He took his phone from the back pocket of his jeans and pushing his glasses nervously up on his nose with his index finger, he dialed a number. With the phone to his ear, he listened.

Princess Saura's focus was centered on the laptop in front of her, but she looked up, concerned. "What's wrong? Why are you pacing back and forth like a panther?"

Aki glanced at his watch. "I'm waiting for Bayani, but he's taking his time. We ought to be going before it's too late."

"Too late for what?" Princess Saura asked.

Bayani walked into the kitchen and scowled impatiently. "Aren't you ready yet? I've got the car outside. If you give me his address, I can put his coordinates into the GPS and we can be off."

"Off where? Where are you boys going?" Princess Saura's attention was now completely aimed at her sons. Her laptop was forgotten.

"It's all right, Mama. Aki wants to see his friend and I've offered to drive him to Cody's flat. And if Cody's not there, well, we can—"

"He's not answering." Frustrated, Aki switched off his phone. "It went to voice mail."

Bayani shrugged. "Then the sooner we find him and speak with him, the better. Shall we go?"

"I don't think that's a good idea," Princess Saura said. "As Bayani said, what if Cody's not there? What if he's somewhere other than his flat? You will have gone there for no reason. And there's no point in chasing all around London looking for him. I think it best you wait until you know exactly where he is, don't you? Your father will be home soon. He'll know what to do."

The thought of his father interfering wasn't a comfort. In fact, it was quite the opposite.

At nearly eighteen, Aki realized he soon ought to be self-sufficient and able to support himself, but the truth was, he was neither. Until he was able to work, he was still dependent on his parents for a roof over his head and for putting food on the table. And for those reasons alone, he had to respect his mother and father. But when it came to Cody, that was another matter. Even though he would like his parents' blessing, he couldn't let them interfere with his decision about Cody.

Cody was out of the ordinary. Someone with exceptional gifts. Look how he'd stepped in to help during the attack in Hyde Park. Not everyone would have been so selfless and so caring. And since getting to know Cody, something deeper and more precious had grown between them. Aki knew he had to get to Cody, and soon, before the chance to correct any wrong slipped away.

"But if I wait, I might lose him," Aki whispered.

He was afraid to speak the words *lose him* out loud in case it happened.

"Lose him? What do you mean, lose him?" A crease appeared between Princess Saura's brows. As if she was confused.

"He might find someone else. He was here and went away with a wrong impression about Bayani and me. I have to explain. I have to tell him we're brothers and not … not *friends* in the way he thinks."

Aki could see his mother now understood the situation. But he hadn't expected her to walk toward him and give him a warm, comforting hug. His mother was never demonstrative with her affections. He knew she loved him, but she had never shown it in such a way before.

"Aki…" Princess Saura sighed. She was taking the time to carefully choose her words. "Aki, my darling. Let me explain something to you. Something I hope you will understand. If your friend Cody is worth fighting for, and if he has feelings for you or perhaps even loves you, then his love won't go away. You won't lose him, not if it's meant to be."

Bayani coughed to attract attention. "Look, I hate to be the practical one here, but perhaps Mama's right. Maybe we should wait until we know where Cody is. Right now, he could be anywhere in London."

Aki ran his fingers through his hair in despair. It seemed his mother and brother were blocking his efforts to get to Cody.

"I know where his flat is. We could go there and see if he'll talk to me."

"Sure, if that's what you want to do. But as Tim said, Cody's probably gone to see his parents. Do you know where they live?"

Aki pressed the keys on his phone and dialed Cody's number again. There was still no answer.

"No, we never spoke about where he came from, but I think his parents live on the outskirts of London."

"The 'outskirts' means he could be anywhere. I think your best bet is to wait. You said he was contracted to play in Amsterdam, so I'm guessing he's signed a contract and can't avoid his commitments even if he wants to avoid you. Which means he has to return to Amsterdam sometime soon. I'm thinking if we can persuade Dad to let you go, why not fly to Amsterdam on Monday and search for him there?"

Aki laughed but it was a laugh of disdain. "Do you really think our father will allow me to go to Amsterdam to speak with Cody? I totally doubt it. Look how he dragged me back to London. Somehow, I managed to get away from these prison walls and the bodyguards, but I'm sure he won't let me leave again. Look how quickly he and Mama came to find me and brought me home."

"Darling, we were concerned for you," Princess Saura said. "That's why we flew back from New York. You know your father and I love you. When we heard you were with this Cody person, we were worried. The security agency contacted us and said that Ron and Tim had some trouble and that—"

"Mother, nothing awful happened. In fact, it was Cody that saved me, and you should be thankful he was there to help."

"And you should never have ventured out, especially to the park in the middle of the night. Whatever were you thinking?"

Aki sighed in frustration. "If you really want to know the truth, I think I was lonely and I needed a friend, so I went to a club looking for one. I thought it was a cool thing to do. And it was sort of all right, but I couldn't find someone I liked. Everyone was … old."

"What do you mean *old*?" Bayani asked.

"Well, they were about your age. They must have been in their twenties or thirties, and that is way too old for me."

Bayani laughed. "I'm glad you realized that. I suppose your *new friend* Cody is a suitable age?"

"It's not funny. And you haven't met Cody so don't knock him." Aki felt an edge of anger building inside. His love for Cody wasn't a joke and it wasn't something to be taken lightly. Bayani seemed to think it was amusing. "That night, I wanted a friend and all I got was a beating. But one good thing did happen. I met Cody. And I don't want to give him up and I don't want to lose him. That's why I have to find him, now before it's too late, and before Papa can stop me."

Princess Saura's strained expression relaxed. "Aki, I will speak with your father. There comes a time when we all must change and perhaps that time is now. There's a point when the traditional things in life are no longer relevant. We live in a modern world and he and I will have to learn to accept that our sons have a need for independence and a right to it. As much as we want to keep you both safe and secure with bodyguards and protection, I realize we cannot restrict you. For now, Bayani has chosen to live in New York, and when the time comes and you have finished your studies, Aki, you must also have the freedom to decide where you wish to live and what you wish to do, and with whom."

"And if I wish to live with Cody?"

"Your relationship with Cody is still new. It's still fresh, and you haven't really discovered one another yet. But if it's Cody you choose to be with, then I promise I will respect your choice of *partner*."

Aki wasn't sure his mother had accepted the fact he was gay, but he was pleased she was willing to try and come to terms with his sexuality.

****

Being in the audience and watching Trend perform seemed strange.

When Aki had worked for Trend, he had either been on stage messing about with the sound and lighting equipment or he'd been out of sight, waiting in the wings for disaster to strike. Luckily, nothing major had occurred. A boom box had been replaced and a new digital mixer was needed, but other than that, everything had been all right.

It was a weird situation to be in. Aki was standing shoulder to shoulder with Cody's fans and he could feel their palpable excitement growing as Trend finished one number and slipped easily into the next. But the fan's loud shouts of adoration were different from the secret thrill he was feeling at seeing Cody again.

He had actually kissed Cody. They had shared a stolen moment of passion together, and he could remember the pleasure and ecstasy he'd felt like it was yesterday. As Cody's hands explored the intimate parts of his body, he had been Cody's for the taking. Only Cody hadn't taken, he had given. And that was something the fans hadn't experienced and he had.

For one brief afternoon, Cody had been his— correction, Cody *was* his—and he wasn't about to lose Cody because of a misunderstanding.

Bayani nudged Aki with an elbow. "Not bad," Bayani said.

"What's not bad?" The noise of the music was deafening and he leaned in toward his brother to hear what Bayani was saying.

"That friend of yours … you did say he was the drummer, didn't you?"

"Yes. That's him."

"Not bad looking, but I wouldn't have said you'd go for a blond guy. I didn't know blonds were your type."

"Neither did I until I met Cody."

Aki knew the routine of Trend's performance by heart. He knew every drum beat, every break, and every planned interaction with the crowd. The concert was coming to an end. The last song on the playlist was being played and as the final notes lingered in the air, Aki tugged on Bayani's jacket.

"Come on. Let's get out of here," he said. "I'll see if we can get to the dressing room before Cody and the others leave the stage. Security might not let us through, but it's worth a try."

Aki headed backstage leaving Bayani to keep track of the twists and turns he made as they headed into the thickness of the dense crowd. Reaching a side door, there were a couple of tough security guards standing at the ready to prevent fans from gaining access to the band, but luckily, one of the guards recognized Aki and allowed them through.

The dressing room was just as Aki remembered it—a chaotic mess. Clothes and equipment were strewn everywhere, but that wasn't what caught his eye.

Standing against a wall was a makeshift vanity table. The band's stage makeup was scattered on top of it, as were the half-drunk bottles of fizzy coke and the half-eaten sandwiches with their dry crusts curling unappetizingly at the edges. Above the table was a mirror, and wedged into the wooden frame was a photo. Aki recognized the photo instantly. It was a printed copy of the selfie Cody had taken on his iPhone when they had exited Madame Tussauds. They had just shared a kiss and their excitement for one another showed clearly in their eyes.

Could it be that Cody wasn't angry with him? Was the photo a sign that there was still hope for their relationship?

The door to the dressing room flew open and in rushed the band. As usual, Mitch was the first to arrive and in typical Mitch style, he headed straight for the sofa and sank down onto it. Brent, Holly, and Sam followed suit and found the nearest available seats.

"Hi, Aki, it's good to have you back. I was beginning to wonder if we would ever see you again." Mitch pulled off his boots and positioned a scatter cushion behind his head. He lifted his feet onto the armrest and laid back until he was stretched full out on the sofa.

Mitch sounded as if he'd half-expected to see Aki in the dressing room and didn't seem fazed by his sudden appearance.

"Hi, Mitch, good to see you too. We're here to see—"

"Yep, I know. You're here to see Cody, and about time. He's been in a funk since he got back from England. What in the world happened while he was there? Anyway, it's none of my business and I suppose it doesn't really matter what went on. You're here now and—"

"And he's about to leave." Standing in the doorway was Cody. Only he wasn't looking at Aki. He was shooting daggers at Bayani and his icy expression said it all.

Chapter Eleven

Cody

Cody hadn't expected to see Aki again, ever. And after the initial shock, he had come to terms with what he had seen and had accepted the fact that his brief, fleeting relationship with Aki was over.

It was clear Aki had looked elsewhere for friendship … for a liaison … for love. It looked like he had found a new boyfriend and Cody had been discarded and left behind. And that was all right. Well, sort of all right. He couldn't dictate how Aki or anyone else ought to feel. It was a free world and Aki was free to do whatever he liked with whomever he liked. But when Cody had seen Aki laughing and messing about in the pool and then getting undressed until he was practically naked with his new boyfriend, the hurt had been intense. He had felt the long, sharp dagger of betrayal strike at his heart. Squaring back his shoulders, he had managed to walk away with his dignity intact but it had cost him a heavy price emotionally to do so. Knowing Aki didn't, or couldn't, return his love was a colossal blow to his self-confidence. Yet, somehow, he couldn't find it in his heart to hate Aki. Aki had a right to choose a lover, it was just a shame the lover wasn't him.

Aki had shown him the way and Cody had been given the chance to express himself and discover his true sexuality and come out as gay to his family and friends. And for that, he would be forever grateful to Aki for being his first love.

Cody looked across the room at Aki and against his better judgment, he felt that familiar twist of hungry desire ignite his loins. He wanted to be close to Aki. To be near him. To touch him, to…

Even if Cody wanted to protect Aki from all the thugs of the world, he knew it wasn't going to happen. Aki now had a new protector—a new lover—and knowing that was like throwing salt on a raw open wound. Cody needed time to heal from the hurt Aki had caused.

"Cody, we need to talk. Now!" Aki looked fierce. As if he wasn't taking no for an answer. "There are things you don't understand. Things I must explain."

"I think it best if you go. There's nothing to say and nothing I don't already know. You've made it clear you've found someone else, only I don't know why you've taken such a delight in bringing him here." Cody pointed a finger at the man standing beside Aki. "Having to see you together … is that to torment me?"

Perhaps he'd misjudged Aki. Perhaps he'd read the signals wrong. When they had kissed, their passion had been intense, and Cody had hoped Aki felt the same way. But apparently, he hadn't.

The boyfriend's hand was now resting possessively on Aki's shoulder, and Aki wasn't objecting. Why would Aki bring his new boyfriend to Amsterdam? Surely, he wouldn't be so insensitively cruel as to tease and taunt?

"You're a fool, Cody Freeman. Can't you see it's you I want, it's you I love, and it's you I need?"

"But what about him?"

"Bayani is my brother. I'm sorry … so sorry for causing any trouble. I never meant to hurt you. You saw something, but it wasn't what you thought."

Cody was emotionally exhausted. His heart was running a gauntlet of emotions. Was Aki offering hope? Was there a chance their love hadn't died? That he had indeed been mistaken.

"What do you mean, your *brother*?"

Aki reached out and grabbed his hand. "Come here, you idiot. You might be used to performing in front of an audience, but I'm not. Where can we go to have a private conversation? I'd prefer it to be somewhere we can be alone."

Cody wasn't enjoying their battle of frustrated love, but it was something he would have to endure if he wanted to discover the truth.

Mitch chuckled. "As the saying goes, I'd suggest you two get a room."

"Not a bad idea," chipped in Sam.

Aki looked at Bayani. "Cody and I are going for a walk. If we're not back in forty minutes, I suggest you either catch the flight home or fetch Tom and Jerry and come and find my dead body. Cody is probably going to kill me for what I've put him through."

Bayani puffed and blew out his cheeks. "No pressure, but if you get into trouble with Drummer Boy, call me. Even if there aren't any problems, just call me to let me know what's happening. I promised Mama I'd take care of you, no matter what."

"I'll be all right," Aki said. And then he smiled and looked reassuringly at Cody. "I mean, *we'll* be all right."

Bayani winked suggestively. "Meanwhile, you two sort things out, and I'll book a hotel room for the rest of the night. Perhaps I'll see you both in the morning."

Things were moving too fast for Cody, but he wasn't about to complain. The sooner he and Aki were alone and sorted any problems they might have, the better.

****

Leaving Bayani and the other members of Trend behind in the dressing room, Cody and Aki left the concert hall and headed for the privacy of Cody's hotel room. They needed somewhere there would be no interruptions while they thrashed out what had gone wrong between them.

"Come on, let's cut through Vondel Park. It's a shorter route back to the hotel," Cody said.

The Vondel Park was a green oasis in the center of Amsterdam. By day, it was a place where tourists and city dwellers flocked to enjoy the tranquillity of the park, and by night, it was a magical place where lovers sometimes met and kissed.

Even though most people were in bed sleeping, there were still a few couples walking the park's lamplit pathways hand-in-hand in the early hours of the morning, and Cody felt the stirrings of longing growing inside him. He wanted to reach out and capture Aki's hand. He wanted to cup his face and plunder his lips with hot kisses. He wanted to…

Aki shivered. "I'll never forget the first night we met. You were there just when I needed you most. If you hadn't rescued me—"

Cody gripped Aki's arm and stopped.

"Don't think about it as a negative experience," he said. "It cost you a few bruises and your phone. But it could have been worse … much worse … and it wasn't."

"You know, when I think about it, the beating and the name-calling were worth it. If it hadn't been for those thugs attacking me, we might never have met. And I wouldn't want to have missed knowing you."

Aki was beautiful, both inside and out. He was petite, fine-boned, and spindly, goofy, also a bit of a geek, but Cody had the urge to smother him with love and protect him from all the evil in the world.

"The name-calling doesn't matter. I agree it's not right and it can be hurtful, but it only shows their ignorance. I have the feeling the world is changing and accepting us—gays, homos, and queers, or whatever they want to call us—for who we are. What I mean is, if Mitch can accept me for who I am, then I believe there's hope."

"What do you mean about Mitch accepting you?"

"Mitch sort of apologized again for his homophobic attitude and told me to go and do my own thing. I think he was saying sorry and offering an olive branch."

"Well, good for Mitch. That's one down. We've now only got to convince the rest of the world that gays and the LGBTQ+'s of this world have a place in society. You don't know how hard it is to be accepted as gay."

Cody shook his head in disagreement. "Oh, yes, I do. Why do you think it was so difficult for me to admit I'm into boyfriends and not girlfriends? It's taken me years to fess-up and you've helped me. Aki, if it wasn't for you…"

Aki shrugged. "You would have found yourself eventually. You might have kept your secret hidden for a while, but you're too honest a person not to come out to the world."

A group of four people, two guys, and two women were heading along the path toward them. Cody lifted an arm and draped it protectively across Aki's shoulders. It seemed like the most natural thing to do, and it was.

The couples passed and nodded, saying "hi" and "*goedenacht*" in Dutch, which Cody took to mean "good night."

Cody with his arm still draped over Aki's shoulders, moved off, and they walked in the direction of the park's gates and the hotel.

"Do you know, I don't know your name," Cody said. "I know it's Aki and that you're a prince, but I don't know your surname. And compared to mine, your life's a complete secret. I don't know anything about you except that our worlds are totally different."

Aki laughed. "You're worried about the unimportant things. To satisfy your curiosity, I am Prince Aki Chan. I'm into geeky things like electronics and the possibility of teleporting objects. I'm also into a musician called Cody Freeman—the end! That's it! Is that enough for you to know, for now?"

"No, it's not." Cody stopped and turned Aki to face him. "I need to know if Bayani really is your brother or are you just playing me?"

Cody's stomach flipped. He wanted to know the answers but he was dreading the truth.

Aki sighed. "You fool. Of course, Bayani is my brother. Stop doubting me, Cody. I thought you could see how much I'm into you. Do you know I love you more with every breath? Now, are you going to kiss me or not?"

Cody hesitated. There were still so many unanswered questions. "Look, I'm new to the gay scene. Can we take it slow? Sort of get to know one another a little better before we dive into a full-on relationship?"

Aki pressed his body close to Cody's.

"Why take it slow? Is that what you really want?" Aki asked. Cody could feel a bulge in Aki's pants that was an unmistakable hard-on. "I'm ready to commit. I want a relationship with you. In fact, I think I *need* a relationship with you … *now*."

Aki's hands were tentatively exploring Cody's body and he could feel a heated passion growing in his loins that matched Aki's. Thinking all hope of being with Aki had been lost, it now seemed there was a chance of finding love. His heart raced with excitement at the possibilities that lay ahead.

Cody moaned his desire. "It's not so much the

committing part I'm worried about. It's more to do with giving our families time to adjust." Aki's searching lips brushed his. He had to keep his thoughts together. He had to get his point across. "Your parents' reaction to us being together is freaking me out. You weren't on the receiving end of your father's anger. I was. He didn't like seeing you with me."

Aki was busy running his slender fingers through Cody's hair and tenderly caressing his cheeks. It was a distraction Cody could do without.

He wanted Aki with a fierce burning hunger, but he had to be sensible. He had to think with his head and not his frantically beating heart. As the older of the two, he knew he had to do what was right for both of them.

"My father wasn't angry," Aki said. "In fact, he was furious, but it was directed at me. I'd left England, and well, I didn't tell him I was going to Amsterdam with you and Trend. He'll be all right and I'm sure he will eventually come around to us being together, and if all else fails, my mother has promised to convince him that you're good for me. And my mother never loses a battle."

"I doubt she'll succeed this time," Cody said and shook his head. "When your father came to collect you from the hotel, I thought he was going to get one of his armed guards to shoot me. You didn't see the look on his face, I did. And what about NASA? You're supposed to be going to America, or that's what you told me. Is that true? Or were you just joking?"

"No, that's true. But it probably won't be for a year or two. I'd like to go to college first, and then I'll consider working with NASA. But that's a long time away. What about you?"

Cody shrugged. "Me? I'll most likely stay with the band for a couple of years and then like you, I'll seek stability and go back to college to finish my studies. I'll still be young enough to start a career in economics if I need to, but meanwhile, I'll have a great time fulfilling one of my dreams—finding stardom and fame as a musician. Basically, I'm uncertain about what's going to happen so I'll just see what life brings and where the future takes me."

Aki's hands were resting on Cody's hips. "But what about now?" Aki asked. "What about us? And more importantly, what about you giving me a proper birthday kiss?"

Cody sensed Aki was teasing. He hadn't been teasing about NASA … no, he was pretty sure Aki was serious when he'd said NASA was interested in working with him. But he was certain Aki was now teasing in a flirting way, and Cody was definitely interested.

"A birthday kiss? Why? When is your birthday?"

Cody knew Aki's birthday was soon, but he didn't know exactly when it was.

"It's tomorrow." Aki looked at the digital numbers on his watch. "Well, actually, as it's nearly two in the morning, I'd say my birthday is today."

Cody smiled. "Then you definitely deserve a kiss from me."

Cupping Aki's face gently in his hands, his mouth descended, and as he captured Aki's parted lips, he heard Aki release a soft sigh of contentment.

Coming up for air, Aki whispered, "I think it's time we go back to your hotel room, don't you?"

Cody nodded.

"Our lives are just about to begin. We are about to start an adventure together."

And then, under the stars, with arms wrapped lovingly around one another, they headed off into the night.

ELIZA DOUGLAS

Evernight Teen ®

www.evernightteen.com

www.ingramcontent.com/pod-product-compliance
Lightning Source LLC
Chambersburg PA
CBHW020621130626
46552CB00003B/1064